WHEN THE
WORLD
STOOD STILL

BOOKS BY KATE EASTHAM

An Angel's Work

THE NURSING SERIES
Miss Nightingale's Nurses
The Liverpool Nightingales
Daughters of Liverpool
Coming Home to Liverpool

KATE EASTHAM

WHEN THE WORLD STOOD STILL

bookouture

Published by Bookouture in 2021

An imprint of Storyfire Ltd.
Carmelite House
50 Victoria Embankment
London EC4Y 0DZ

www.bookouture.com

ISBN: 978-1-80019-488-5
eBook ISBN: 978-1-80019-487-8

To all nurses and health care workers who staffed the front line during the COVID-19 pandemic.

I had a little bird,
Its name was Enza.
I opened the window,
And in-flu-enza.

1918 children's playground rhyme

CHAPTER 1

St Marylebone Infirmary, London

Late September, 1918

The afternoon light came in gently through the leaded glass of the Infirmary chapel, brightening the white starched cap of the probationer nurse who knelt on the hard floor with her head bowed in seeming humility, her hands clasped in prayer. Emily Burdon was furious, so furious that two bright spots of anger burnt on her cheeks and the streak of red at the front of her dark brown hair appeared to gleam with extra fire.

It just wasn't fair, she had done everything right for her patients – so many new men, soldiers back from the front still in their grimy uniforms and mucky boots. She'd been busy all morning making sure they were welcomed, their observations done, some history taken and that they were comfortable in their beds waiting for doddery old Dr Jessop to do his ward round. And she'd spent ages with poor Private Sid Wilkins, a nineteen-year-old so badly shell-shocked that he couldn't stop shaking and gibbering and crying. She'd done all of this and more, and yet just because she'd broken another glass thermometer – this time slipping from her grasp as she rushed to help a man who was about to fall out of bed – Sister Montgomery had given her a dressing down in front of the whole ward and told her that the cost of the thermometer, and the one she'd broken yesterday, would be deducted from her wage. She'd been sent off the ward, to come here, to the chapel, to pray that she would learn not to rush around the ward or be so clumsy. Not to rush around the ward! Had Sister even seen how many new admissions they were getting each day? They were short-staffed already with the war, never mind the nurse who'd gone off sick with a fever.

Her knees were hurting now on the tiled floor, but still she knelt, using the pain to try and salve her anger. She needed to be calm when she got back to the ward – Sister would give her one of her sharp looks as soon as she came in through the door, and if she didn't look repentant she might be sent back up to the chapel. She didn't have time for this; there was still plenty to do to make the new admissions more comfortable. Damn Sister Montgomery, her stupid, old-fashioned ways and her enforcement of them when a war was raging through Europe and young men – including Emily's own fiancé, Lewis – were risking their lives. The whole country had to bear so much sorrow, including the probationer nurses, the lowest of the low in Sister's eyes.

Emily had kept her engagement secret from all but her close friend Lucy. She didn't want to risk any aggravation from senior staff members who still fervently believed that a nurse must give her whole life to the profession, that there was no question of having a boyfriend, a fiancé, a husband. When she married after the war, she'd have to leave. It broke her heart to think about it – she loved the work and now that she was in her final year of training, she knew unequivocally that she could make a difference for her patients. But she also knew that to be a complete person, she had to have a man in her life. The innocent fumblings and kisses that she'd shared with Lewis so far had quickened her blood and made her breathless. There was so much more to discover – and judging by the amount of time she spent thinking about it, she was certain that she wanted to explore all of it. For her, nursing could never be the ultimate sacrifice.

Using the pew in front to pull herself up, she gave each leg a good rub before straightening and gazing, as she always did, at the statue of the Madonna and child. She loved the pale blue of Mary's gown and the angle of her head as she gazed lovingly at baby Jesus. She liked to imagine that she would look just like that if she had a child, even though she knew that the reality of motherhood wasn't quite so blissful.

Ready to make a move, she took a deep breath, pulled her apron straight and slipped out of the pew. When she reached the door, she glanced back and smiled at the Madonna as she stood, immutable, bathed in September light. She was ready now. She could go back to the ward with a pious face and follow orders without question, all so she could make sure that the injured soldiers received the absolute best of care.

Just inside the door to the ward, Emily met Private Sid Wilkins, who was still in his dusty, battle-stained uniform, torn at the elbow. He was trying to light a smoke with shaking hands, his eyes flitting about wildly; the poor man was haunted.

Sensing he was about to walk off the ward, she called out to him, 'Sid?'

He looked up for a second and she noted a twitch at the corner of his mouth.

'Where are you going?' she said, placing a gentle hand on his arm.

He shot back away from her, as if he'd been stung, and started muttering a jumble of angry words. 'Get down!' he shouted as she moved closer, throwing himself onto the floor, crouching, trying to shield his head. As she came closer, he reared up and shot his arm out, dragging her violently down onto the floor with an almighty crash. The noisy ward went instantly quiet and then the distinctive tap of Sister's leather heels sounded on the wooden floor.

In that moment, she didn't care that Sister was on the approach – Sid was shaking with fear, lost in some terrible flashback. She'd jarred her wrist when he'd dragged her down, but she righted herself instantly, desperately trying to soothe him.

The clip of Sister's heels fell silent, but Emily had eye contact with Sid now and didn't want to look up. As he cried, big tears rolling down his face, she knelt next to him, her arm around his shoulders, telling him over and over that he was safe, that no one was going to harm him.

Once she felt the terrible trembling of his body start to settle, she risked a glance up to Sister. Her thin mouth was pressed in a determined line but much to Emily's surprise the woman's grey eyes were full of sympathy and she was gesturing for Emily to help the young soldier up from the floor.

As soon as Emily had him on his feet, Sister came to his other side. 'Now, young man, you're perfectly safe with us. Let's get you into bed, you'll feel a lot better if you have some rest.' They walked carefully down the ward, as the murmur of conversation and the usual hum of activity started to resume around them.

'You'll be all right, Sid!' called an older man with thinning hair, one sleeve of his uniform hanging empty. Lance Corporal Bill Steadman. When Emily had admitted him, he'd told her his tragic story – he'd been hit by a shell whilst trying to save his mate and it had blown his right arm clean off. He'd been lucky to survive with no other injuries, though that didn't make his suffering any easier.

Sid was compliant as they tucked him up in bed, gratefully slipping between the sheets, still in his tattered uniform. Emily had tried many times to persuade him to exchange it for clean pyjamas but he'd become more and more agitated with each attempt.

'Stay with him until he's properly settled,' Sister counselled, reaching out a hand to straighten the pillow beneath his head. 'I'll go up to the clinic room to get some medicine to help soothe him.'

'Yes, of course,' Emily said, glancing after Sister as she moved up the ward, checking the beds on either side as she went.

*

It was soon time for lunch and as Emily walked beside Nurse Sitwell, one of the senior staff nurses, on her way to the dining room, she heard the sound of running feet behind her and a familiar voice calling, 'Emily, Emily!'

'No running in the corridor, Nurse Bennett,' called a stern voice.

'Sorry!' shouted her best friend, Lucy, breathless.

Nurse Sitwell frowned and indicated that she would continue to make her way alone.

Lucy was almost doubled over, gasping for breath, her jet-black hair spilling out from beneath a cap that had slipped sideways. For a moment she couldn't speak. 'Have you heard?' she gasped.

'Heard what?'

Lucy straightened up and then blurted it out, 'They're going to let our group of probationers pass early, because they're so short of trained staff.'

'What? Do you mean we won't have to take the test?'

'Yes, Dorothy just told me! In a few weeks' time, we'll all be trained nurses.'

Emily felt stunned. She didn't want to admit it, but she couldn't help but feel a little disappointed… She'd already been revising for the test and she was hoping to pass with flying colours – and make her parents and her two sisters proud.

'Say something,' Lucy demanded.

They were still in the corridor with staff streaming around them on their way to lunch. When yet another nurse side-stepped them and tutted, Emily got hold of her friend and dragged her into the doorway of the doctors' mess.

'Well… I suppose it's a good thing, but it will feel strange, not having to complete the last few months and do the test.'

'Oh, you'll get over it!' Lucy grinned, her eyes round with excitement. 'And it means I don't have to spend hours and hours slaving over books, I can just go straight through with a free pass, get rid of this itchy dark grey uniform and receive my hospital badge.'

It still troubled Emily – not that she wanted to spend *hours and hours* studying, but there was something to be said for feeling that you'd earned your place.

'You'd have been fine anyway,' Lucy rambled on, 'you've always been quick off the mark. But I'm not like you, the written stuff takes a long time to lodge in my thick skull.'

'You haven't got a thick skull! You are very—'

'Excuse me,' a man's deep voice interrupted.

They both looked up together and even Lucy was stuck for words. A broad-shouldered man in a black three-piece suit and immaculate white shirt stood in front of them. His thick chestnut hair was brushed back from his face and he had an amused glint in his startlingly blue eyes. 'Sorry to interrupt, nurses,' he said, his voice vaguely American, 'but is this the doctors' mess?'

The tiny wrinkles at the corners of his eyes turned up when he smiled and for a few moments they both failed to comprehend what he had just said.

'Oh yes, sorry, it's right here,' Emily indicated.

'No need to apologise,' he replied, his eyes still shining. 'I'm Dr James Cantor, a new recruit to your surgical team, I'm meeting Dr Jessop in the Mess.'

'Yes, of course,' said Emily, grabbing Lucy's arm to be on their way. Lucy was red in the face and struggling to supress giggles as they walked away with Emily shushing her, desperately trying to stop her friend saying out loud what she herself had already been thinking.

CHAPTER 2

In the low slant of September evening light, the St Marylebone Infirmary appeared warm and inviting. An array of yellow brickwork, ornate windows and pointed towers, accessed through an impressive archway which ran beneath the Infirmary chapel; the whole place was designed to provide succour for the souls of the staff who worked there, and the many desperate people admitted as patients.

Alma was delighted by her first impression. As her taxi cab drove through the archway, its solid tyres bumping over the cobbles, she held onto her hat until the vehicle ground to a halt outside the main door to the hospital. The driver glanced at his meter and then jumped out, ready to unload her large leather suitcase.

She took her time, deftly adjusting the hat that she'd bought specially – its single curled green feather toned perfectly with her eyes and matched the fitted jacket that clung to her narrow waist. She took up her leather purse and opened the cab door, remaining inside the vehicle for a few moments with only her dark blonde head peeping out, as she savoured the elegant lines of the hospital's architecture.

The driver doffed his cap as she slipped him his fare, plus a handsome tip, and he offered to carry her valise, but she wasn't sure where she was going as yet and knew that she could easily manage by herself. After all, she'd grown up riding horses through the Virginia backcountry, she'd worked as a nurse in a field hospital on the Western Front, and, more importantly, she'd just spent six weeks living with her maiden aunt in Knightsbridge; she could manage anything after that.

As the cab rumbled away, Alma glanced around to get her bearings. She needed to find out where the quarters for trained staff were and, no doubt, she would need to meet up with the Home Sister. She'd try the main entrance first, see if she could get directions.

As she strode confidently towards the door, it swung open and a very handsome, broad-shouldered man in a black suit appeared. He had a slight limp, which made him even more intriguing.

Pausing momentarily, she decided to make herself known to him by asking for directions. 'Excuse me,' she said, depositing her suitcase smartly on the ground. 'Do you know where the nurses' home is?'

'You're American,' he said smiling, his own accent denoting some place across the Atlantic, but where, she wasn't quite sure.

'Yes! How *did* you guess?'

'I've no idea…' he said with a wry smile, reaching out to shake her hand, 'I know you'll be wondering about my accent, so I'll put you out of your misery – I'm Dr James Cantor and I'm from Prince Edward Island, Canada.'

'Ah, of course, that's it, a Canadian.'

'Yes indeed. And I'm afraid I'm new here today too, so I can't give you reliable directions. But if you go in through that entrance, I'm sure there'll be someone who can help.'

'Why, thank you,' she said, wondering if he was perhaps a little too staid for her taste after all. *But it would certainly be interesting to find out…*

Alma picked up her suitcase, carrying it easily. She had a good feeling about this placement already and hoped that the interior of the hospital would match up to what she'd just seen on the outside.

Met by the sight of a straggly group of rather grim-looking families clustered in the entrance hall, she did begin to wonder what might lie in store for her. These poor souls were all undernourished, their clothes were ragged and one of the women had a dry, hacking cough. But a sweet little girl with bare feet, a grubby face and a head full of blonde curls, looked up and gave her a shy smile that lifted her spirits.

'You've managed all sorts since you came over here to join the war effort,' Alma murmured to herself as she walked along, 'you can manage this as well.'

A young woman with dark eyes and a frown that belied the good humour of the upturned corners of her full mouth was walking briskly in her direction. Alma knew instantly from her purposeful demeanour that she had to be a nurse.

'Excuse me,' she enquired, 'can you direct me to the nurses' home?'

'Yes, of course,' the girl replied with an English accent that Alma couldn't quite place, but she spoke well, and she appeared friendly. 'Come with me, I'm just on my way back. I'm a final year probationer – Emily, Emily Burdon.'

'Pleased to meet you Emily, I'm Alma Adams and I'll be working as trained staff on the military ward, as of tomorrow… and oh, as you can tell, I'm American.'

'That's good!' Emily said enthusiastically. She had a smile that lit up her face and made her look even more beautiful than she already was. 'I mean not that you're an American, that's good as well, of course it is. It's just that the military ward is where I'm working… and I do need to warn you, it's non-stop on there at the moment, we're packed out with soldiers.'

'Oh, that's OK, I'm not long back from a stint at Ypres so it should be familiar territory for me.'

Alma couldn't help but feel a warm glow when she saw the girl's eyes widen with admiration. She was genuinely pleased to have met someone so quickly who seemed so nice. It always helped to have a friendly face around, even if the nurse was still a probationer. And this Nurse Burdon, she certainly looked like she might have a bit of something about her.

*

'I've just met a new staff nurse – she's American and she's moving into the trained staff quarters. And guess what, she's going to be on my ward.' Emily burbled as soon as she was in through the door of Lucy's room.

'What, two Americans in one day?'

'Well, we don't know if that doctor was American or not, do we, but yes, two in one day.'

Lucy pulled herself upright, her pale face glowing in the dim light and her grey eyes wide, smiling a welcome even though Emily had only been gone about fifteen minutes. She patted the bed next to her, 'So, did you get a letter from Lewis, then?'

'Oh yes, I forgot…' Emily pulled the letter out of her pocket before snuggling up next to Lucy on the bed. 'I'm sorry there wasn't any post for you.'

'Oh, don't be sorry, it'd only be me mam complaining about things and telling me about next door's chickens or what my sister and the nephews have been up to. Life goes on very much as before in the rural backwater where I'm from.'

'Yes, my lot are much the same,' Emily said, starting to read her letter, noting that Lewis's pencil scrawl was much more untidy than usual and the lines on the page were all over the place.

'Mmm, he's saying the usual things, they're all working hard, he can't wait to see me, he'll be on the move again soon. Oh, and one or two of the men have gone down with a fever, some kind of flu that they get at this time of year. And when he comes home on leave, he doesn't want to go back home, he wants to come here, to London.' Emily sat quietly for a moment, still staring at the letter. They'd had so many wrangles over this particular issue – he never wanted to go home to their village and she always did.

Lucy put an arm around her. 'Well, from what you've told me about that father of his, I suppose we can understand why he doesn't want to spend too much time at home?'

Emily nodded and let out the breath that she didn't even realise she'd been holding. 'Well, there's not really any point thinking about it, who knows when he'll get leave anyway.' She didn't know if it was meaningful or not, but each time she got a letter from Lewis, she felt it drain her. The war had gone on so long, and far from the acute feeling of imminent danger it had been at first, it all now felt like some dull, exhausted grind. She knew that Lewis had little fear for himself – he'd always had a strong nerve, the first to do everything, even when they were children. So what she was feeling wasn't fear, not any more – it was a persistent grievance that had caused regular disagreement between them. Lewis never wanted to go home when he was on leave – he preferred to stay in London, while she always wanted to see her family, not just because she would feel guilty if she didn't but because she missed them, even after all the years away.

'Try not to worry, Ems. It should all be over soon, anyway,' Lucy continued, giving her shoulders a squeeze. 'And then you and Lewis can get yourselves properly sorted out.'

Emily felt her body stiffen and she scrambled up from the bed. She wanted him to come back, of course she did, but there was also a part of her that worried about it happening. It would sound heartless if she said it out loud, so instead she offered, 'I just wish he'd come home now, this whole thing has gone on far too long, hasn't it?'

Lucy sighed. 'You're not wrong there… And we've seen what it can do to the men who survive. Those who've been sent back… most of 'em will be damaged for the rest of their lives.'

Emily felt a jolt. Lucy was always 'to the point' and said things that other people would leave unsaid. But still, Emily knew from the last few times that Lewis had been home on leave that he definitely wasn't the same carefree young man who'd gone off to war with such a swagger. It made her sad, thinking of that tinted photograph of him in his uniform that she'd laughed and cajoled him into having taken before he left home. She'd had to move it off her dresser because it brought tears to her eyes – Lewis there in the photograph, staring out at the camera with his blue eyes and boyish grin. That bright, handsome young soldier with a lock of pale brown hair falling rakishly on his forehead who had pulled her close and kissed her tenderly before he left for the front line. She wasn't sure now with the distance of time, maybe it was only half-remembered, but she was sure that he'd clung to her then, held onto her as if he never wanted to let her go.

'Are you all right?' Lucy's voice broke through, 'I was just saying about the men… how they're affected by the war.'

Emily felt her skin prickle. 'Yes, yes, they are struggling… they just need some more time to get back to normal, that's all,' she said emphatically, desperately trying to convince herself as she pushed the letter firmly back inside her pocket.

They continued to sit in quiet companionship, Emily content with murmured conversation as Lucy took up a new dress that she'd been trying to sew some buttons on for days, gasping and then giggling as time after time she stuck her finger with the needle.

'Give it to me,' Emily said in the end, 'you'll have blood all over that frock.'

As Emily finished the job, Lucy got up and wandered absent-mindedly around the room, tidying up and preparing her uniform for her late shift the next day. When the light had dimmed even more and the corridor outside was hushed, she whispered, 'Thanks, Emily, for saving the day again. I do love you, you know that don't you?'

'I love you too.' Emily kissed her on the cheek and handed Lucy her dress before slipping out of the door with a contented sigh.

CHAPTER 3

The new American nurse was already on the ward deep in conversation with Sister Montgomery by the time Emily arrived, breathless. She'd overslept and been forced to run along the corridor, feeling a hole in the heel of one stocking with every stride. Her friend, Grace Malone, a newly qualified nurse, moved up so Emily could squeeze in beside her. As Emily settled in, relieved to see Sister was still occupied, Grace reached up to tuck a straggle of loose hair behind Emily's ear. Grace's curly red hair was cut short, forming a golden halo around her head, and with her pale blue eyes and beatific smile, there was something almost otherworldly about her. She was, without doubt, one of the kindest nurses in the hospital and Emily always thought of her as a guardian angel.

At last Sister and Alma finished their conversation. Emily couldn't help but think how clean and stylish Alma looked in her light grey uniform and spotless apron, her waist nipped in by a black belt with an ornate buckle and a shiny hospital badge pinned proudly to the bib of her apron. Emily was transfixed and still staring when Alma looked up. She offered the new nurse a small smile but Alma narrowed her eyes and then looked away. Sister Montgomery pursed her lips and frowned in Emily's direction.

Emily felt Grace take her hand and give it a squeeze – Grace had told her many times that Sister always had one nurse whom she targeted, and all Emily needed to do was keep a low profile until it passed. But that 'low profile' evaded Emily every single day – she always seemed to be in the thick of every incident and even if she wasn't directly responsible, it was her name that Sister called.

'For those of you who don't already know,' Sister announced, puffing out her chest, 'this is our new trained member of staff, Nurse Adams. She not only comes direct from working as a volunteer at a field hospital in France, she also has the highest of recommendations from the prestigious Virginia Training School in America. We have much to learn from her so please, nurses, do pay attention.'

Emily watched Alma carefully; she was almost smiling, not smug exactly, but somewhere close.

'Nurse Burdon!'

Emily instantly pushed back her shoulders as Sister called her name.

'I trust you are paying attention?'

'Yes, Sister,' she called, with as much conviction as she could muster.

'Once we are through the report, I want you to go straight to theatre, another nurse has gone off sick and they need someone to help out. And this time, do try to keep the instruments in order, Dr Jessop has never fully recovered from your haphazard presentation of scalpel, scissors and forceps.'

'Yes, Sister.' Emily nodded, knowing that the remark was unfair. She'd been thrown in at the deep end that first time; Theatre Sister had been away and they were, as always, running on skeleton staff because of the war. And Dr Jessop's mumbling instructions hadn't helped either. She felt like telling Sister this and that she'd made sure to revise her instruments and theatre procedures; she'd even practised the routines with Grace so that if she was called again, she would be confident.

Emily listened intently to the ward report. Served by a very sharp memory, she already knew the names and diagnoses of all of the patients but she was particularly interested to find out how

Sid Wilkins had fared overnight. Once Sister had finished, Emily murmured a 'see you later' to Grace. She wanted to get straight down to theatre and make sure that she was on top of things before the first patient came through the door.

As she turned from the group, she caught Nurse Adams's eye; her lips were pressed in a firm line and she was holding up her index finger, indicating for Emily to wait. *Wait for what?* Emily wondered. Still Nurse Adams was holding up her finger. Emily felt her cheeks flush with anger. *Who the heck did this new nurse think she was?*

She felt Grace reach for her hand and then she heard her whisper, 'Don't take it personally, she's an experienced nurse, she's just trying to make her mark.'

Finally, Nurse Adams nodded towards Emily as if to say, *You can go now.* Emily tried to control the look that she gave in return, but she could see by the way that Nurse Adams widened her eyes and glared with equal fire that no contrition had been conveyed. The gauntlet had been thrown down.

'I'll have a word with her, nurse to nurse,' murmured Grace as Emily slipped away from the group.

Emily could feel the beating of her heart as she strode briskly down the corridor. She knew, of course, that Nurse Adams was senior and she had to be subject to her orders; it annoyed her, it always had, but all probationer nurses had to accept it as a fact. But now that she was almost qualified and she had become firm friends with Grace, apart from Sister, she'd been on the receiving end of less and less of that hierarchical nonsense. But if the American was up for a fight, then she would be ready. Only it was strange that when she'd met her in the corridor yesterday, she'd seemed so completely different – Emily had even thought that they might become friends.

At least the annoyance had removed most of her nervousness about going into theatre, though she still felt a flutter as she pushed open the polished wooden doors to the hallowed space that contained two operating theatres. The sharp smell of carbolic hit her, triggering a stab of anxiety. *Would she remember everything?* She gritted her teeth and breathed in the carbolic. Of course she would.

'Are you the nurse who's been sent?' a crisp voice uttered.

Emily's heart jumped a beat; it was Theatre Sister, her generous curves squeezed into a stiff uniform and large apron cinched at the waist with a buckled belt. Emily noted a pair of sharp, steel scissors pushed into her belt, ready for use. She opened her mouth to reply but Sister was already issuing orders. 'Get yourself ready – scrub your hands and then don a theatre gown and a mask,' she said, pointing to the door of the changing room. 'You'll be working with one of the new surgeons today. I would have liked to have supervised him myself but Dr Jessop has requested specifically, after some experience with a probationer a few weeks ago, that he only work with senior qualified staff.'

Emily nodded and took a deep breath.

The patients were coming in through the door on trolleys by the time she emerged and she reminded herself that she was calm, perfectly calm. She saw Lance Corporal Bill Steadman on one, all trussed up in an operating gown with a cotton turban on his head. 'Hello there,' he called, reaching out his left arm to grab her hand. 'I'm glad to see a friendly face… They've brought me back to "tidy up" the stump, that's what they're calling it. Jessop told me there's still some dead meat on there that needs to come off.'

Emily caught the whiff of an odour from the stump bandage; she'd not done the dressing herself for a few days but she'd already noted that there were some areas of necrotic tissue.

'It'll be straightforward,' she said, easing into her stride as she always did when she had contact with a patient. 'And it'll mean that the arm can heal properly.'

'Ha, what's left of it!' he said, his voice brittle and overloud in the high-ceilinged theatre. Emily walked beside the trolley as the porter wheeled Bill through. There was still no sign of the new surgeon but the anaesthetist, Dr McKenzie, was in position, readying the mask and the chloroform.

'You know the drill,' she reassured Bill. 'They'll put you to sleep first and then when you wake up it will all be done and you'll have a new dressing and bandage in place.'

'Aye, I know, but I'll be sick as a dog, I always am with the anaesthetic.'

She heard the door open and the sound of the surgeon's voice greeting Dr McKenzie – it was the American she'd met briefly in the corridor yesterday. Emily felt her heart skip a beat – how very ridiculous. She was in the thick of it, for goodness' sake; she needed to focus on the work at hand.

She helped the porter to transfer Bill onto the wooden theatre table. 'I'll just go and check that we're all set,' she said, giving Bill's hand a squeeze, 'I'll be back in a minute.'

Dr James Cantor had his back turned at the sink, scrubbing his hands with carbolic soap. Emily checked the instruments on the trolley; thankfully, Sister had already laid them out correctly and covered the tray with a sterile cloth. All seemed to be in order and an enamel bowl was on the floor ready and waiting to receive the used swabs.

Emily went straight back to her patient, who was quietly drifting off to sleep. She couldn't help but feel for him as he lay so helpless on the table and she began to unravel the bandage from his upper arm. He'd told her some of his story – how he'd volunteered as soon as war was declared, and being older than the rest, it had been hard to leave his wife Agnes and their two children. He'd met Agnes on the upper deck of an omnibus on a glorious summer's day and they'd married six weeks later. She was his life. But he'd been swept up with war fever and everybody had said it would all be over by Christmas, and so he'd whistled his way down the street with his fellow recruits, not wanting to miss the opportunity to do his bit. But after what he'd seen out there in the trenches, and the years and years of living like that, he'd said it had almost been a relief to get blown up in the end – at least now he knew he had a chance of survival.

Emily swallowed hard. She'd seen his wife visit with their two tousle-haired boys, she'd seen the love that they had for him. She would do everything in her power to help save him. She would make sure that every bit of rotten flesh was removed from his stump, and that it was cleaned properly and sprayed with carbolic.

She went straight to the sink to scrub her hands for the final time. Dr Cantor cleared his throat and she looked up. 'Please can you fasten my gown, nurse?'

She dried her hands quickly and stepped behind him, reaching up to tie the strings.

'Thank you,' he said, turning to face her. 'And you are?' His voice was so warm it made her smile.

'Nurse Burdon – Emily,' she replied, immediately aware that she'd blabbed out her first name, something that was never done, especially if you were a probationer.

'Do you want to get yourself some sterile gloves… Emily?' and in that moment, as he looked at her with those tiny upturned wrinkles at the corners of his eyes, she was sure that he recognised her even though she was wearing a mask.

As she pulled on the thin rubber gloves, he examined the wound. 'We'll just open up and have a better look at what's going on inside, what do you think, Emily?'

'Yes, good idea,' she said, making sure that she wasn't flustered as she handed him the scalpel.

As she watched him make the first assured incision, she felt calm – she could see his expertise from the way he handled the knife. 'Hmmm,' he said, peeling back the skin and then glancing up as if for approval, 'I'm not going to mess about cutting away bits and pieces, the end of the bone looks like it's been affected. We need to cut the whole thing back and give this fella a fresh start. Do you agree?'

'Yes, I think that's a very good idea. Even the smallest bit of infected tissue can lead to further suppuration. We could wash the area out with some dilute carbolic acid or eusol solution as well?'

'Good thinking.'

She was relishing being a part of this already – after her first disappointing experience in theatre she'd never thought that the work could be so engaging. And even when he asked her to pass the saw, when he was ready to trim back the bone, she was only a little daunted. She made sure to grit her teeth, as metal snagged bone, until the job was done.

Once the wound was washed out with Emily's antiseptic solution and the edges of the incision were sutured, Dr Cantor held the dressing pad in place whilst she applied a stump bandage. This application was one that she'd practised many times; bandaging was her forte, at least that's what her tutor had said. In no time at all, she had the bandage tethered exactly in place and secured with a new safety pin.

'Well done, you bandaged the hell out of that – I think that would survive another shelling!'

Emily tried not to feel self-satisfied, she didn't want to get too above herself – they already had another patient waiting and who knows what might be required – but she was beginning to feel that theatre work might well end up being another forte of hers.

Unfortunately, Sister stepped in to immediately dispel her growing enthusiasm. 'Dr Jessop has been called to an urgent case on Female Surgical and he will be away for some time. I will be taking over here with Dr Cantor…' Emily saw Sister smile graciously in his direction. 'So, you can go back to the ward right away.'

Was that a shadow of disappointment she caught in Dr Cantor's eyes? Alas, there was nothing she could do but strip off her rubber gloves and her theatre gown, wash her hands, and go. At least she could console herself with knowing that she'd be able to make sure that Bill Steadman was safely back on the ward and settled in bed.

Grace whisked her away as soon as she was in through the ward door. 'Come with me. I need you to keep out of Sister's way for a while, she's just found another broken thermometer and even though you've been away all morning, she thinks you're responsible.'

'But that's not—'

'I know, it's not fair, but you know what she's like. I need to do Private Wilkins's dressing, and you're about the only one who can keep him calm.'

Not wanting any trouble, Emily quickly grabbed a wooden screen and trotted after her. 'Did you see Nurse Adams scowling at me during report? I don't suppose you've managed to have a word with her?'

'She wasn't exactly scowling, Emily,' said Grace evenly. 'And I haven't managed to speak to her, not yet…'

'Don't worry, I will, it's not fair to ask you to do it…'

When they reached Sid Wilkins's bedside, she held his hand to keep him calm. She spoke to him as Grace cleaned the wound and applied a fresh dressing and he didn't even flinch, his medicine had made him so sleepy. Emily would have loved him to shout out, or pretend to be in agony like some of the men did just for a laugh, but Sid… he never moved an inch. Such a young man should be telling stories about his exploits, not lying helpless and sedated in a hospital bed. The shrapnel wound on his chest was fairly superficial and seemed to be healing; it was minor in comparison to other physical wounds on the ward, but Emily doubted if Sid would ever make a proper recovery. He was broken on the inside.

She exchanged a resigned look with Grace as she helped pull his tunic back into place. 'I know, it's sad,' Grace murmured, 'but

I do know that Sister is trying to get him a place at one of those special hospitals that deal with shell shock...'

'Is she?' Emily replied bleakly. She'd never heard of any soldiers coming back from those hospitals and she didn't know what they did to the patients in there. And the thing was, for most of the nurses, once you had someone under your care, you wanted to see things through, try to make a difference, do anything that you could to help. If a patient died unexpectedly or went out through the door in just the same state or in a worse condition, it was hard to accept. The nurses were there to make patients better, not see them lie helpless and suffering.

'Come on, let's get on and do some more dressings.' Grace gestured up the ward where Sister was deep in conversation yet again with Nurse Adams. 'She's really taken with our new American colleague, isn't she? I think it might be safe for you to put your head above the parapet.'

Towards the end of the shift, as more patients returned from theatre, Emily had the satisfaction of seeing Bill come round from the anaesthetic and start to take sips of water. He hadn't even been nauseous this time.

'I'm gettin' used to that stuff,' he said groggily, reaching over with his hand to feel tentatively at the stump. Emily told him exactly what they'd done in theatre and reassured him that all of the 'bad meat' had well and truly gone. He gave her a bleary smile and a big tear ran down his cheek, 'Thank you, Nurse... you make me feel like I'm still worth something, even like this.'

'Of course you are... And you've got your wife and your two lovely boys who love you dearly.'

He was sobbing now. 'I told Agnes I just wanted to die, let her move on. But I love her so much... and the boys, even with me like this, I can't...'

She took his hand. 'You have a family, you have something that's worth fighting for. Never, ever, give up.'

Swallowing hard to stop herself from crying, she patted his shoulder and then straightened the sheets on his bed, fussing over the detail to make him feel even more cared for. 'Now you get as much rest as you can, we're going to get that arm of yours healed properly this time and then you're going home to your family.'

'Yes, Nurse,' he sniffed.

Seeing Nurse Adams alone at last, Emily took a deep breath and walked briskly up the ward. She told herself that she needed to stay calm, that after all, the American was senior to her, but that didn't stop her cheeks from starting to burn.

'Excuse me, Nurse Adams, do you have a moment?' she asked politely, making sure to keep her voice even.

'Yes, of course, Nurse Burdon isn't it?'

'Yes,' Emily replied, meeting her level gaze with a determined one of her own. 'I'm going to be straight with you—'

Nurse Adams almost took a step back, but then she smiled and Emily could see a steely glint in her eye.

'I didn't feel that you were being altogether fair this morning, when you prevented me from leaving the group at report. I had explicit orders to go directly to theatre.'

When Nurse Adams didn't reply, Emily tried not to say anything else. She knew that was the wisest course of action but, as always, her heart ruled her head and she came straight out with it. 'I know that you are a qualified nurse and you are very experienced, but, as a matter of fact I have now almost completed my own training and I've been working on this ward for two months, I know it back to front.'

Still Nurse Adams didn't speak but Emily could see two spots of high colour clearly defined on the woman's cheeks and her green eyes were fiery.

Undaunted, Emily continued to hold her gaze, keeping her head high – again, something that was probably not a good idea, but she was used to holding her own during the numerous spats that had been part of her growing up with two sisters.

At last Nurse Adams breathed and she dropped her shoulders 'I don't want any trouble with you, Nurse Burdon – Emily – and after our initial meeting in the corridor yesterday, we do seem to have got off on the wrong foot. I apologise if I was heavy-handed, but Sister had told me that I had to be extra-vigilant with the probationers and she singled you out in particular as being 'headstrong'… I can see now that she was right on that score at least.' She smiled now and reached out a hand. 'And that is the reason why you are definitely a nurse that I want on my side… so please accept my apology.'

Emily was taken aback for a moment; she hadn't expected such a whole-hearted response and she was impressed by Nurse Adams's directness. 'Apology accepted,' she smiled in return, reaching out to shake her hand.

'And please, Emily, when Sister's not around, do call me Alma.'

'Yes, of course.' Emily replied, delighted to sense the return of that early rapport they'd shared during their first meeting in the corridor.

Later, as she walked back to the nurses' home with Grace, Lucy came dashing up behind them, out of breath as always. 'What a day! We had so many admissions on Female Medical, all bad chests and fevers… that flu that we had in the spring, it seems to be back with a vengeance.'

'I hope not.' Emily linked her arm. 'Ugh, you do smell strange and your apron is grubby.'

'I know, sorry, I didn't have any time to change my apron. One poor woman was coughing so much she vomited. She was covered in grime when she came in – it's terrible, people have no choice but to live in such poverty… but I cleaned her up and tried to make her comfortable. She begged to keep her daughter with her, said there was nobody else at home to look after her. Her poor little girl has big sad brown eyes, she was desperate not to be parted from her mother. But Sister said no, the girl had to go to the children's ward… They sent for that new porter and he had to carry her away screaming. He was in tears, said he'd rather be in the trenches than doing work like this.'

'The poor little mite,' said Grace. 'My sister, Molly, she's seven and she never leaves Ma's side.'

'I was like that too,' Emily added, 'I pretended to be all tough, but I always needed to know exactly where my mother was. I wasn't bonny like your Molly though – with her lovely blonde hair and dark eyes.'

'Ah yes, you saw her that day when she was waiting outside for me. She looks like a little angel but she's not always sweetness and light, she's got a real stubborn streak. Did I tell you that she had a fist fight with her older brother and gave him a black eye?'

'No!' Emily laughed. She loved to hear stories about Molly; being the youngest of her own family she could relate to some of the mischief that she got up to.

'Are you ladies going back to the nurses' home?' a voice called from behind. They all turned as one. 'Yes,' Grace chirped. Emily opened her mouth but didn't speak and Lucy murmured, 'Is that the new American?'

'Yes,' Emily whispered back to her.

'Nurse Burdon,' continued Alma seamlessly, coming alongside Emily to take her arm. 'I'm sorry that we didn't have more time to speak on the ward. Sister has monopolised so much of my time.'

Emily heard Grace hold back a small gasp.

'That's all right,' soothed Emily, 'we did have our little chat so that's all that matters.'

'Yes, indeed! First days are hard aren't they and it can be easy to read things wrong.' Then she launched into a story about her first day as a probationer at the hospital in Richmond, Virginia, talking non-stop and giving all kinds of detail, including her fine cotton uniform with watermelon pin stripes – it sounded so exotic that Lucy sighed with envy.

Suddenly Alma fell quiet and Emily heard Lucy suppress a giggle. Dr Cantor was striding down the corridor towards them. She was about to open her mouth to say hello but Alma, cool as a cucumber, was there first, dropping Emily's arm and instantly greeting him, 'Why James, we meet again, how was *your* first day?'

The three of them exchanged an astonished glance as they kept walking, leaving the sound of Alma's tinkling laughter echoing in the tiled corridor behind them.

'She's quite something, our American nurse,' Lucy mused, and then she whispered in a gentle mock American accent, 'Why James, we meet again…'

Holding hands, they picked up speed, trying to hold back snorts of laughter as they burst out through the door, and ran towards the nurses' home.

Back in her room, Emily leant against the closed door for a few moments. Her heart was still pounding from the exertion and she felt something else, something new – her whole body was tingling. She pushed herself upright, kicked off her shoes and sat on her neatly made bed to strip off her stockings. She'd been irritated all day by the hole in the heel of her stocking, on top of which her feet were always throbbing when she got back from the ward. The only thing that helped was a long soak in the bath. But she'd have to wait; Lucy had gone first and she always took ages.

Emily stood up, removing her apron and letting it slide onto the floor with the discarded stockings. After spending a whole day making sure that starched bed sheets were exactly straight and corners were folded just so, it always felt good to leave her uniform in an untidy pile. She'd be forced to clean it up before morning, but right now it pleased her to let it lie.

Walking over to her mirrored chest of drawers, she took the pins out of her hair, scattering them on the polished wood. She shook her hair free and it tumbled in natural waves down her back. Staring at herself in the mirror, she ran her fingers through it and as she swept it back, the streak of red dispersed, producing a natural highlight to the dark brown locks that she'd always been told were her crowning glory. Both her mother and her two sisters were fair and she'd always felt a bit left out when she was younger, but now she enjoyed the difference. Everybody said she took after her father. Five years ago, he had suffered a stroke that had taken the right side of his body and most of his speech, she could hardly remember what he'd been like before.

Sighing, she stared back at herself in the mirror. It made her feel sad, thinking about how a strapping man in his late forties, a busy shopkeeper, full of life, had been struck down in a single moment. Her father was well cared for at home, but it still broke her heart to see how sad he looked sometimes. It was a good job her mother was always looking on the bright side, still treating him like she always used to, teasing him, trying to make him laugh. It made Emily smile now, thinking of his lopsided grin. It seemed even in the darkest of situations, there was always some little bit of light if you looked hard enough to find it.

CHAPTER 4

It was only a matter of days before Alma was walking back from the ward as part of the group. With her winning smile, confident ways and the amusing stories that she told so vividly of her time as a mischievous probationer at the Virginia hospital, they were all a little in love with her. And it seemed that Emily was perhaps a favourite of Alma's. Alma would often link her arm first, before any of the others, then turn to her to ask something and they'd soon be deep in conversation. Emily truly hoped that Lucy hadn't noticed – they'd always had a special bond and she didn't ever want Lucy to feel excluded. That's why Emily had refused Alma's kind invitation to accompany her to Knightsbridge on a visit to her maiden aunt, Alma Foster. In any case, Alma had just told them that her aunt was coming to the nurses' home that evening instead.

Alma had asked Emily and Lucy for moral support as she scurried around making hurried arrangements.

She shot out of the visitors' room, looking decidedly flustered for the very first time since they'd known her. 'I arranged for some cake to be delivered from the hospital kitchen, there's still no sign of it and she's due any minute.'

'I'll go,' Emily volunteered. 'If I can't get cake, I'll ask for some sandwiches.'

'Thank you,' Alma breathed, her cheeks burning pink.

As Emily slipped out through the main door, she saw a taxi cab pulling up. She quickened her pace, not wanting to risk meeting the aunt head on. Alma had told her that the woman was not only formidable but she could take an instant dislike to people.

There was no cake – the cooks had been struggling for supplies – but at Emily's request they hastily prepared a selection of paste sandwiches. No one ever knew exactly what the paste was – it was best not to enquire – and the edges of the dark, gritty war bread were worryingly ragged, but they had no choice, there was nothing else. Aunt Alma would have to like or lump it. Emily smiled to herself, thinking of her mother's stock phrase as her fussy middle sister, Lizzie, sat at the table pulling her face at whatever was on her plate, whilst Alice, the eldest, sat stoic and unflinching, quietly eating whatever was put in front of her.

Emily was so intent on delivering the sandwiches that she almost bumped slap bang into Dr Cantor as he moved swiftly in the opposite direction. She levelled up the plate in the nick of time as the precious food slipped sideways.

'Sorry,' he murmured, politely stepping around her. And then turning on his heel, 'Oh, it's Emily, isn't it? I didn't recognise you in your own clothes.'

She looked down at the fitted black skirt and green blouse with embroidered collar. 'Oh… er yes,' she said. 'Of course. No uniform.'

He was still looking at her.

'All safe, thank goodness,' she breathed, gesturing to the plate of sandwiches, 'Alma's aunt is paying a visit. She's expecting cake, but these will have to do.'

'Mmm…' He frowned, leaning in to inspect the sandwiches. 'Not sure about that bread, I've heard it contains grit and potatoes, and from what I've heard about the English aunt, she's very exacting in her preferences.'

'Well, let's hope her preferences include wartime paste sandwiches… and, if they don't, well, as my mother would say, she'll have to like it or lump it.'

'Like it or lump it, I'll remember that one!'

As she approached the door to the visitors' room, Emily could hear a murmur of stilted conversation and what sounded like Lucy's nervous giggle. She glanced sceptically at the sandwiches, knowing full well there was no hope that this meagre offering would go anywhere near to rescuing the situation. *Best to go in smiling*, she thought to herself, taking a deep breath before pushing open the door. As she entered, she held the plate aloft with both hands, as if it was some prized gift.

'Ahh, you must be Emily,' the aunt pronounced, catching her with a very direct gaze.

'Yes, pleased to meet you,' she said, returning the gaze, before placing the sandwiches on the low table in the centre of the room. 'And I'm so sorry but the kitchen staff weren't able to run to cake, but they have sent these…'

'Thank you, Emily,' said Alma, her voice tight, 'I was just telling Aunt Foster that you're from the North of England.'

'Yes, I'm from a small rural village in Lancashire.' She smiled politely.

The aunt's expression remained resolute as she sat straight-backed on an upholstered chair that seemed woefully inadequate to her requirements. 'I see, Lancashire… I don't know anything about Lancashire,' she said witheringly, indicating that she would like to try one of the sandwiches.

Emily wasn't going to be dismissed so easily so she rushed to help. She lifted a sandwich onto a side plate and took it straight over, leaning in close enough to smell the woman's lavender scent and see the specks of face powder that settled in the lines around her mouth. 'Paste sandwich?' she smiled, giving Aunt Alma no choice but to take the plate. Then she sat down determinedly beside her and started to talk, relentlessly, 'Oh, but Lancashire is wonderful, you must visit if you get the chance – we are a very industrious county, famous for our cotton mills and agriculture, and the countryside is so beautiful and virtually undiscovered – green fields, wild flowers, ancient woodlands and of course, the moors and the fells.'

'You make it sound so enticing,' said the aunt, her icy smile starting to thaw a little as she took up a knife and sliced the sandwich into two neat triangles.

Emily forged ahead with her conversation, 'What part of the country are you from?' She could feel Lucy and Alma relaxing as she monopolised the aunt's attention.

'Oh, I was born in Derbyshire as a matter of fact, not far from where your esteemed founder of modern nursing, Florence Nightingale, spent her early years. And then we moved to London, for father's work, and that's where my sister, Millicent, Alma's mother, was born. She was much younger than me, quite a reckless girl and of course my father indulged her terribly. She ended up going on some extravagant trip to Virginia and that's where she met and married Carl Adams, Alma's father... an *American...*' She glanced over to Alma, trying to catch her eye, but her niece was seemingly engrossed in conversation with Lucy. Aunt Foster didn't flinch, and as she looked directly back to Emily with a decided glint in her eye, she announced loudly, 'Alma is an only child. She's always been in danger of being thoroughly spoiled.'

Emily was scrabbling for something to say as the aunt's words hung in the air. With a small smile playing around her mouth, Aunt Foster aimed a gaze as sharp as an arrow directly at Alma. Emily could see Alma's cheeks burning bright red but she never lifted her head from her conversation with Lucy. Taking a deep breath, Emily reached for her tea and took a big swig, placing the cup back in the saucer with a decided clatter.

'Tell me about Derbyshire, Miss Foster, is it very beautiful?'

When there was no response to her question, Emily ploughed on with a further description of the Lancashire countryside and the Bowland Fells in particular. She caught a swift look of grateful thanks from Alma as the aunt launched back into more chit-chat.

'Oh yes, there is also the most wonderful countryside in Derbyshire and just thinking about it now takes me back to my girlhood… I was born during the Crimean War, just after Miss Nightingale departed with her brave nurses. They named me after the Battle of Alma…'

As the aunt continued to talk about the war and then her bucolic childhood on a large country estate, much to her surprise, Emily found herself genuinely interested. She was drawn into a world that was so far removed from her own that it seemed fantastical. There was a subtle air of sadness about Aunt Alma though… some past tragedy, maybe the whisper of a broken engagement? Emily was hoping that she could keep her talking long enough to get to the nub of it.

Almost as if she caught Emily's train of thought, the aunt turned swiftly to Lucy and Alma. 'So my dear, are there any eligible bachelors at the hospital?' Lucy's eyes widened like saucers.

'Oh Aunt,' Alma sighed, shaking her head.

Undaunted, the aunt leant forward in her chair. 'You need to be getting a move on, my dear, you're not getting any younger.'

Lucy coughed on her tea and needed to take out a handkerchief to dab at her mouth.

'I know all about you modern girls and your shenanigans – what with votes for women, shortening your skirts, marching in protests and chaining yourselves to railings. You all seem to think that those are the important issues of the day but—'

'Aunt, with respect, we are in the midst of a world war. For many women of my generation, marriage is the last thing on our minds – we are working as nurses, police officers, architects, you name it… The world has changed, things have moved on.'

Aunt Alma sighed. 'One day you will regret that attitude, I know you will. You should be actively looking for a suitable match.'

Alma give a wry smile. 'Oh I've been trying out various possibilities, no need to worry about that. The only thing is… I've not found any man who can match me.'

The Aunt's ample bosom rose sharply and her cheeks reddened beneath the thick powder; she looked like she might be about to explode inside her strongly whale-boned corset. Instead, she took another sip of tea, and turned back to Emily and crooned, 'But you, my dear, you have a rare beauty. You will have no problem whatsoever in securing the heart of any young man.'

Emily opened her mouth to speak; she was about to disclose, perhaps unwisely, that she was in fact already engaged, but fortunately the moment was lost when an urgent knock sounded at the door and Home Sister Mary Kelly appeared. Her hair was as white as her cap but her face pink with agitation.

'So sorry to interrupt,' she said, out of breath, 'but there's been some incident on the military ward and they need a nurse to go urgently.'

Emily jumped up from her seat. 'I'll go,' she gasped, 'it's probably our patient with shell shock, he must be in one of his agitated states… It was so lovely to meet you, Aunt Foster.' Emily briefly shook her hand and didn't give her the chance to reply before she ran from the room.

Even before she reached the ward, she could hear a man first shouting, then keening like an animal in pain. It went right through her, making her heart pound and her legs move even faster.

As she arrived, Dr Cantor and Sister Montgomery, with her frilled cap knocked askew, were struggling to restrain the patient but, much to her surprise, it wasn't young Sid Wilkins – it was Bill Steadman.

Emily ran towards them. 'What's going on?' she cried out.

'This poor man has just heard that his wife has died,' Dr Cantor said, matter-of-factly, still holding onto a wild-eyed Bill.

'Get off me!' Bill shouted. 'I need to go home, I need to be with Agnes!' And then he was wailing again, that terrible sound, and he fell to his knees in the middle of the ward.

Sister Montgomery was forced to let go of him and Bill curled over, a tragic figure, still wailing. Emily gestured for Dr Cantor to release him and she crouched down beside Bill, speaking softly to him, saying his name. He glanced up and began to wail even louder.

Emily was not afraid of his grief. She stayed with him, there on the floor, with her hand resting lightly on his back. 'Bill, I'm so sorry to hear the news about your wife.' He shot a glance at her, his eyes terrified. His face was swollen with crying; he was exhausting himself. 'I'm so, so sorry,' she murmured again.

He was nodding now and wiping the back of his hand across his eyes. Sensing that he was ready to stand up, she helped him, supporting him as he stood swaying. Out of the corner of her eye, she saw Dr Cantor step towards them. Without looking in his direction, she held up a hand, gesturing for him to keep his distance.

'Can you walk?' Bill nodded. 'Come on then, let's go down the ward, there's an empty side room, we can go in there and you can tell me what happened.' He nodded again and with Emily's help he was able to move.

Once inside, Bill slumped down on a chair, shaking his head from side to side, starting to visibly sag as the last of the fight seeped out of him. Emily knelt beside him; there were no words that she could say to soothe him, she knew how much love he had for his wife, this was terrible news.

'What happened to Agnes?' she asked at last.

He stared at the floor as he recounted the story, his voice flat. He told her that his wife had started with a fever two days ago – she'd sent him a note saying that the children had just had some bug and she'd picked it up, that she wasn't well enough to come and see him, but she'd be back next week. He hadn't thought much about it. Then this evening, out of the blue, he got a note from their neighbour, a Mrs Starmer, she said that Agnes had become gravely ill with a cough and a fever, all in the space of a day, and that she had died.

'I'm so sorry, Bill,' Emily repeated, standing up now and placing an arm around his shoulders. He was nodding and he wiped his eyes with the back of his hand. Then, abruptly, he shot up from his seat. 'I have to go home, now, tonight, I need to look after the boys – our neighbour has them but she has her own family, they can't stay there, not for long.'

'I don't think you can go anywhere tonight, Bill,' Emily said. 'You need to be careful, you've still got the stitches in, remember?'

'I have to,' he said, trying to push her out of the way.

'Listen to me, please, just for a moment,' she said, standing firm and raising her voice just a little. 'We have to work out what's best for you and the children. We can't have you running off into the night, and seeing you as bad as this won't help your boys. They'll be asleep by now. If it makes you feel any better, I'll go along to your neighbour's house – right now. And in the morning, if all is well, we can take out the stitches and get you ready for home. But you have to wait till the morning, Bill. What use are you going to be to your boys if that stump gets infected again?'

He was still shaking his head but there was less fight in him now.

'Once I've checked on them, I'll come straight back to the ward and tell you how they're doing. You have to agree, Bill; it's the safest plan, for you and for your children.'

'All right, nurse, all right,' he gasped. 'I'll do it, if that's what you think is best. You've always looked after me, I trust you to do what's right…'

'Good man, now, tell me what your boys are called?'

'Mattie and Tom,' he said, his voice breaking again as he spoke their names out loud.

Once he was back in bed, Emily went to find Sister Mont-gomery. She was at her desk, writing up notes, a tuft of steel grey hair still straggling from where her cap had been displaced, but she was otherwise collected and her gaze was piercing as always. 'Yes, Nurse Burdon?'

Emily cleared her throat and came straight out with her plan.

'I'm not sure you should be going off into the city alone at this time of the night,' Sister said, pursing her lips. 'Can you not leave it till morning?'

'It's the only reason that Bill agreed to stay, I have to do it.'

'Do what?' Dr Cantor asked, appearing at Emily's shoulder.

'She wants to go and see Bill Steadman's boys at his neighbour's house… I don't like the idea of it, not at this time of night.'

Dr Cantor's reply revealed the ease he had with Sister already. 'I'm finished here for now, I can go with her.'

Sister Montgomery raised both her black eyebrows and then switched her bright gaze to Emily, letting a pause hang in the air for a moment before she spoke. 'Well then, I think we have our solution, Nurse Burdon.'

It felt strange to be walking through the city with Dr Cantor at her side. She hadn't even had time to go back to the nurses' home to explain. She hoped that Alma and Lucy wouldn't be worrying over why she was taking so long, but there wasn't much she could do about it – Sister had thrown a shawl around her shoulders and Dr Cantor had removed his white coat and off they'd gone. Neither of them knew London, so one of the porters had given directions. Emily had memorised them so she was the one leading the way, but she had to walk briskly to keep up with the doctor, who moved at some pace, despite a pronounced limp, which she'd never even noticed before.

Neither of them spoke as they walked along Exmoor Street, quiet now with only a few passers-by and the occasional taxi cab. Emily spotted their next turn and led them through various other streets and alleyways with that sense of urgency that only a mission like this could bring. 'This must be it, yes that's right?' she murmured to herself. They turned down a narrow street that was poorly lit by gas lamps and, as brave as she was, Emily was grateful for the tall, broad-shouldered figure of the doctor beside her. 'Right,' she said, peering through the gloom, only just about able to make out the house numbers. Seeing a property with dark, forlorn windows, she felt a stab of sadness. 'That must be Bill's house, number eight. Therefore this has to be the neighbour's, number ten. Do you agree Dr Cantor?'

'Yes, you seem to have led us to the right spot,' he said. 'And please, Emily, do call me James.'

Emily felt an unexpected jolt of pleasure, and she couldn't help but smile as she walked purposefully towards Mrs Starmer's front door and knocked firmly.

The door opened almost immediately and a middle-aged woman with dishevelled hair stood before them, holding a hand to her chest. 'Sorry,' she said, 'we've had a terrible shock today… and I thought you were someone else.'

'We're from the hospital – I'm a nurse looking after Bill Steadman and this is his surgeon, Dr Cantor,' Emily introduced them. 'Are you Mrs Starmer?'

'Yes, I am,' she said, her eyes wide with concern.

'No need for any further worry,' Emily said steadily. 'We are here on his behalf… He's suffering terribly and he's in shock, so we promised him that we'd check on Mattie and Tom and start to make arrangements for Bill to be discharged home tomorrow.'

The woman began to breathe more easily again, reaching up a hand to tidy her hair, 'Well, it's very good of you both coming out here to check on us, you must be so busy with all those sick patients. You deserve a medal, you surely do.'

'Oh no, really, it's fine,' James and Emily murmured together as Mrs Starmer gestured for them to come in.

A warm fire flickered in the grate of the one room downstairs and although the space was cramped, as far as Emily could see in the lamplight, it appeared to be clean and comfortable. A man stood up from his chair by the fire and offered his seat.

'No, it's quite all right, we don't want to disturb you.' Emily replied. 'The only way that I could get Bill to agree to stay in hospital for one more night was to promise that I'd check on his boys and let his neighbours know what was going on.'

Two small boys with dark, curly hair were sleeping on a settee in the corner of the room; their faces looked clean and pink. 'There they are, the poor little mites,' said Mrs Starmer, 'They cried themselves to sleep, exhausted they were. I've got four of my own upstairs so I put these two down here and it's best, so we can keep an eye on them. It was awful what happened today… it was the eldest, Mattie, who came runnin' with his little brother clinging to his hand, saying Mummy was asleep and she wouldn't wake up. I told them to stay here and my eldest took care of them while I went in next door. Oh, it was terrible, poor Agnes was lyin' there on the floor, she must have fallen over and couldn't get up. She was still clutching her rosary and I could tell that she was dead right away… I mean, I knew they'd all been sick over the last week with a bad cough and such, and I was praying that it wasn't that bad flu. At the school this week they've had children falling ill at their desks, just dropping down where they sat. I'm going to be keeping mine at home till we know what's happening… What is this? Could it be that bad flu?'

Emily could see a frown line between James's eyes. 'I couldn't possibly say for sure, but we've been hearing more reports of cases in London and in France amongst the soldiers and we've started to get admissions at the hospital. Those who contract it can fall severely ill within hours and die rapidly,' he said steadily.

'Oh my goodness!' Mrs Starmer pressed her palm to the centre of her chest. 'But Agnes was just a young woman and such a good mother to those two boys, she was strong and full of life, why her, how could she have died? It's often only the oldies or the infants who die from the flu...'

'Sadly, that doesn't seem to be the case with this one... In fact, it is young, healthy people in the prime of their lives who are most severely affected.'

'But that's terrible,' groaned Mrs Starmer. 'We need to pray that this thing doesn't take hold proper.'

The man who'd been sitting quietly in his chair by the fire spoke up then. 'I haven't wanted to worry anybody, but I've been reading about it in the paper. The King of Spain went down with it and at the Vatican, they've even suspended collective audiences with the Pope.'

Mrs Starmer narrowed her eyes, taking it in. 'So it's not just here then, it's all over the place.'

There was a moment of quiet in the room broken only by the spit of the fire and the gentle breathing of the sleeping boys. And then, as if knowledge of the flu being worldwide had somehow made it more manageable for Mrs Starmer, she brushed back her hair with a determined hand. 'Well, you can tell Bill not to be worrying, we'll keep these boys here with us for as long as he needs.'

'Thank you,' Emily replied, 'but from what he's been saying, he definitely wants to come home tomorrow. He could probably have done with longer to make sure that his arm is properly healed, but I think in these circumstances it's best.'

'Rightly so, I suppose. But how a man with one arm is going to look after two lively children, well, we'll have to see won't we... There will be the funeral to organise as well, of course. I sent my eldest to get the police and they arranged to take Agnes away, but there will be all sorts of stuff to manage.'

'Please take this,' said James, pulling some money from his pocket. 'It's for the boys, give it to Bill tomorrow.'

'That's very kind of you, Doctor, I'll make sure he gets it. He's a proud man is Bill and he wouldn't have taken it from you. But he won't have any choice if I give it to him.'

A shiver went through Emily as the door to the house clicked shut behind them. It seemed darker now in the street and with all that had happened she felt hollowed out. They walked quietly side by side, both lost in their own thoughts. Towards the end of the street, outside a house, there seemed to be some commotion. A young woman was crying and clinging to a small child. The door stood open and as they passed by, they could see the shrouded body of someone being brought out of the house on a stretcher. Emily shuddered and exchanged a glance with James. This didn't feel like a coincidence. There was something decidedly off about the whole thing. Emily pulled her shawl more tightly around her body and, without thinking, she slipped her arm through James's and held on tight.

CHAPTER 5

Armentières, France

November 2, 1918

A ghostly evening light illuminated the sky, traced by red and yellow flares revealing silhouettes of ruined buildings and splintered trees. Sergeant Lewis Dupree clung to the wheel of the motor ambulance as the vehicle lurched along a rutted road. Hitting what felt like a boulder, the solid tyres were thrown off track, sending the ambulance perilously close to the rim of a huge shell hole. Lewis swore loudly above the rumble of the engine, crunching the gears and wrenching the steering wheel back into line as a thin mist of exhaust fumes invaded the vehicle.

'That was a close one!' he yelled, slapping the thigh of the ashen-faced young soldier in the passenger seat. Private Benjamin Simms, assigned to his very first mission, sat rigid in his seat, unable to reply.

Abruptly, they came to a halt and Lewis jumped down. 'Come on, Ben,' he shouted to the wide-eyed soldier, his blond hair just visible beneath his new tin hat. 'Just watch your step, there might be unexploded shells anywhere around here.' Seeing the lad's instant shock, Lewis struggled to keep a straight face – he always felt for the new recruits but couldn't help but tease them, just to see the look on their innocent faces. He must have been just as naïve when he was first posted but he couldn't recall being quite as earnest or as terrified. But it all seemed such a long time ago now.

As Lewis reached into his breast pocket for his smokes, his fingers caught the edge of a folded envelope – a letter from Emily, his fiancée, which he'd forgotten to read. He placed the cigarette between his dry lips, feeling irritated now. For the first time in ages, he was yearning to go home, needing to be in the arms of a woman. Seeing Ben stepping gingerly across the churned ground lifted his spirits though; he wouldn't let it go much further, but he was still enjoying his joke.

Before he could light up his cigarette, the shape of a man with erect posture and wearing an officer's uniform appeared and a sharp voice cut through the gathering darkness. 'Are you the transport?'

'Yes, sir. Sergeant Dupree, sir,' Lewis replied, quickly slipping the cigarette back into his pocket.

'Now listen up, Sergeant,' said the officer, dropping his voice a notch. 'This is a special assignment and I want you to keep it quiet, do you understand?'

'Yes, sir.'

'We have a number of sick men who need to be moved to an emergency hospital… at this location,' he said, passing over a piece of paper. 'Load them up as quickly as you can. There've been all kinds of rumours spreading about this damned fever – *la grippe*, they're calling it. These stories are bad for morale, so your job, Sergeant, is to transport the men and keep your mouth shut. Understood?'

'Yes, sir,' Lewis repeated, wondering what the hell he'd got himself into now.

'The men are all gathered in that abandoned trench,' the officer said, pointing with his baton as he walked away. 'My own sergeant – Jackson – he will help you load them.'

Lewis took a deep breath, needing that smoke more than ever now. 'Come on, mucker,' he called to Private Simms, who stood rooted to the ground. 'Did you hear that?'

'Yes, Sarge,' Ben nodded and started to move.

They could hear the men coughing even before they got to the sand-bagged rim of the trench. Lewis glanced back to Ben and twisted his mouth with concern; this wasn't good. He'd heard the rumour as well. It was no joke, men were dying from this flu.

'Try not to get too close to 'em,' he offered, seeing Ben's stricken face. 'We'll be all right if we don't get too close.'

As soon as they were down by the men, Lewis knew that his advice was futile. A couple of the lads were able to stand and climb out of the trench unaided but others were so weak that it took Lewis, Ben and Sergeant Jackson to move them. One strapping fella on a stretcher was breathing loudly, a rasping in his chest; it wasn't easy to see in the light, but his face looked dark and there seemed be froth coming out of his mouth.

'This poor lad isn't going to make it,' Jackson murmured.

'Why haven't they moved him sooner?' gasped Lewis, unable to hold back his outrage. 'The poor bugger can hardly breathe.'

'He only fell ill this morning,' said Jackson, exchanging a very sombre glance with Lewis.

'Jeez…' Lewis breathed. 'No wonder they want to keep this quiet. This is worse than being shelled.'

Once the men were loaded, Lewis had a quick few drags on a cigarette and a hefty swig from his hip flask before jumping into the driver's seat. He took a torch out of his pocket and glanced at the map the officer had given him – the destination was out of the way, close to the cemetery. He felt a stab of pain, knowing that it was no accident where the hospital had been sited.

In the back, the men were all coughing – a dry hacking cough. Lewis saw Ben take a handkerchief out of his pocket and hold it across his nose and mouth.

'Good thinking.' He nodded, wishing he could do the same, but he needed both hands on the wheel to drive this lot back over the rutted road.

'Right lads,' he called to the men, 'you'll soon be safe and sound at the hospital. There'll be some lovely nurses to look after you and the good news is, you'll all be back home to Blighty in no time at all.'

Normally, comments like that would raise a cheer from even the most hardened of Tommies, but there was no response from the men in the back – just the wheezing of breath and that terrible, deep, hacking cough, cough, cough.

*

A few days later, Lewis was lying flat on his back on a makeshift bed in a crowded hospital tent. In the next bed lay Ben – he'd been complaining of a terrible headache for a full day before he'd spiked a fever and started with a cough. At first, Lewis had deluded himself that it was only normal for the young soldiers to catch something when they first came up to the front line – the lad was only eighteen, no more than a child, and he was bound to pick up an illness or two. But it hadn't taken long for Ben to be fighting for each breath and then Lewis had started with the worst headache of his life – he felt like his head was bursting and his whole body ached, he was as weak as a lamb. All he could do was lie down. He hardly dared look at Ben now, but he could hear him fighting for every single breath.

When Lewis did steel himself to glance over to the bed, his heart almost stopped – the lad's lips were blue and his face was dusky and one hand lay helplessly on top of the white sheet. Lewis rolled over onto his side, tears stinging his eyes. The boy had only come up to the front last week. A hard lump of anxiety caught in his throat – whatever was going on with the men now, it had to be taken seriously, the *grippe* was a killer. Lewis had never properly prayed, not in his whole life, but he launched into a heartfelt mix of words for himself, Ben and all the other men groaning and gasping their last in this lonely tent far from home.

He must have fallen asleep eventually, because when he rolled onto his back and glanced again to the next bed, Ben was gone. A cold shudder went through his body. Already, there was another soldier in the bed and he too was coughing. Poor Ben, he was no more than a kid, and now he'd joined the list of all the other young soldiers whom Lewis had got to know and then lost – including his best friend, Jim Ashworth, who he'd joined up with. Lewis fought back the memory of that particular loss every single day. And there'd been Des, another lad he'd got close to... He'd been shot through the legs and caught on the wire. All night long he'd shouted for help until his voice had grown weak and then just as light dawned, he'd fallen silent. Something had broken inside of Lewis after that. That's when the nightmares had started. He'd wake up screaming, cold with sweat. He hadn't slept properly for years; if it hadn't been for the liquor in his flask he would probably never sleep again.

Des had been the first to ask Lewis to go and see his mum, if anything happened to him. Ben had done the same after less than a week on the front and he had written down his mum's address in London. Lewis had said yes automatically, never thinking that he would be contemplating it so soon. But even at the time, he'd known he wouldn't go. How could he? Since Des, all the young men he got pally with had asked him the same thing – there were dozens of them and even if he could remember their mums' names or their addresses, he couldn't possibly visit all of them. And, in truth, he had to think about himself; even if he wasn't the next one to snuff it with this flu, he had enough mess of his own to clear up.

Just thinking about his own situation made his stomach burn with acid, not helped by the fact that the day before he got sick, he'd had a heavy night of drinking and playing cards with a bunch of Tommies – who had been unaware of his trademark sleight of hand. He'd been pleased with himself – he'd managed to bag a good few bob and three packs of cigarettes, which even as he fell sick, he'd made sure to bring with him in his kit bag. He sat up in bed as the acid surged up from his stomach, burning at the back of his throat. He could feel his skin hot and sweat drenched his body in waves, but his own cough was just a tickle compared to some. He reached for the pack of cigarettes beneath his pillow and lit up. He needed to stay calm. Still lying on his back, he breathed out and watched the smoke curl up to the peaked canvas of the tent. Every single morning, the bugle sounded as they buried more bodies in the cemetery up the road; he'd have to find a way out of here as soon as he could if he was to have any hope of survival. He'd heard that some of the sick men were being moved up to the hospitals on the French coast and Lewis knew that he needed to make sure that he was on that convoy.

A young nurse ran past his bed – some poor bugger had got himself out of bed and he was ranting and raving, trying to stagger his way out of the tent. She looked a bit like Emily, with her dark hair swept up loose beneath her cap. He was glad he'd written to her weeks ago to tell her about the fever spreading through the camp. It was useful, her being a nurse – maybe he could write to tell her that he was sick and ask if she could get him moved to a London hospital, or even the one that she worked in. St Marylebone was a good place and he now knew plenty of people in London. Since he'd joined up and left the village where they'd both grown up, he'd seen a fair few places, broadened his mind.

He smiled to himself, thinking of this new life that he would have away from the village forge where his father was the blacksmith. He intended to stay away from there permanently if he could; it was no fun being the only child of a downcast mother and a brutal father. When he was just seven and his father had held him down on the floor with a red-hot iron, fresh from the forge, inches from his face, he'd vowed that one day he would leave and never come back. He'd have to work on that with Emily though – she was close to her family, and she'd always said that when they were married, she'd want to go back up North and live near to them. He knew that she was hoping he'd change his mind and every single time he had leave, they'd have a row over it. Some of his friends had said he should dump her, do his own thing, but he had to have Emily – she'd always been the brightest and the best-looking girl in the village, there was no way that he was going to leave her behind.

The final drag on his cigarette set him off coughing and it racked his thin body. He threw the stub onto the ground and leant over the side of the bed as he fought for every breath. He felt the pain of it deep inside his chest. When at last he brought up some phlegm, he spat it straight out onto the earth floor.

'Sergeant Dupree?' It was Sister's voice – he knew he might be in trouble.

'Sorry, that was a bad one,' he croaked, reaching out a hand to accept the square of cotton cloth that she proffered.

'How many times do we need to tell you men, you must not spit on the floor.'

'Yes, Sister, understood,' he croaked, mustering his contrite voice. But she was already moving to assist another young nurse who was fighting to help a soldier, a big strapping fella who was coughing and delirious and struggling to get out of bed.

Lewis made himself sit up at the side of the bed. He needed to look like somebody who would withstand a journey in an ambulance train to one of those hospitals on the coast. This tent was a place where people died, and he didn't want to have any part in that. Forcing himself to stand, even though his legs felt like jelly, he made himself walk to the door of the tent. He leant there for a while, looking out at the ruined landscape. Increasingly, there'd been rumours that the war was almost over, *any day now*, the men were saying. With the deathly sight in front of him – the twisted metal buried in the bare earth, the barbed wire and dead stumps of trees – and the sick and dying coughing their guts up behind him, he couldn't help but wonder what it had all been for.

CHAPTER 6

St Marylebone Infirmary, London

November 10, 1918

The ward was crammed full of men coughing; they hardly had any wounded coming through now. This flu was terrible, a respiratory condition much worse than anything that even Sister Montgomery, with all her years of experience, had ever seen. Notices had gone up around the city warning of the dangers of spitting and telling people to cover their mouths and noses if they coughed or sneezed and to wash their hands. People were wearing masks in the street.

There was very little time for Emily or any of the nurses to think about the dangers of their work as they battled daily to save lives. This was no mild fever with a cough and a sneeze – soldiers, young men in the prime of their lives, were coming through the door already cyanotic, with blue lips and fingertips. Once the nurses saw this sign, they knew that it was too late for these patients. Sadly, they were already lost.

Emily ran down the ward towards a patient who was hanging out of bed and sounded like he was choking. His lips and face were blue and his terrified eyes were staring, unseeing, right at her. He was only a young lad, much too young to be gasping his last breath. She pushed him back onto the bed, pulled down her cotton mask so that he could see her face and grabbed his hand, speaking to him, saying anything that might help to soothe him. She said his name, Lucas, desperately fighting back the tears when she saw his eyes darken as the last heaving, choking breath left his body.

Sister Montgomery was there in a moment, next to her at the bedside. The flu epidemic had caused a transformation in her. She no longer fussed over tiny details – and of course, there was no question of anyone being targeted for minor misdemeanours, not any more. Sister threw herself into the nursing, working harder and longer than any of them. No one would have wished for a pandemic, but the good, the unexpected light, that rose to the surface could feel humbling.

Sister gave Emily's arm a squeeze. 'Are you all right, Nurse Burdon?' she asked quietly.

Emily swallowed hard. 'Yes, Sister,' she replied. She was ready, she knew exactly what was needed of her next. She would make sure that Lucas was washed and had a label around his neck to identify him, she'd wrap his body and tie him into a sheet, and get the porters to move him from the ward as quickly as possible. The bed would then be disinfected and immediately made up to receive another male admission.

At a bed opposite, Alma was fighting to keep a delirious man with a fevered crimson face in his bed. Emily pulled her cotton mask back into position and went to help. Before she could get close enough, the patient swung out his arm and caught Alma across the face, knocking her cap askew. 'I'm all right!' she cried, pulling her cap back into position. 'I'm just worried he's going to hurt himself.'

'Come on, soldier, let's have you back in bed,' Emily told him authoritatively. He looked at her and saluted.

Alma shook her head as if in amazement at Emily's abilities. 'I'm so glad some of them are still listening to orders.'

'Are you OK? Let me have a look at your face?'

'It just feels a bit bruised that's all, we haven't really got time anyway… Once I'm sure this one's going to stay in bed, I'm going up the ward to try Sergeant Dawson with some heroin cough mixture, and if that doesn't work I'll mix him another whisky and hot water.'

Emily walked quickly back to Lucas's bed. Seeing his lifeless form sent a stab of pain through her. But she needed to get on with the laying out so that she could make room for more patients. The nurses could never give up – maybe the next one would pull through.

They were putting in twelve-hour shifts now, day and night, so when their work came to an end, the corridors were full of exhausted young women trudging silently back to the nurses' home. By this time, Emily felt broken inside, dried out, not even capable of tears, as she concentrated on putting one foot in front of the other, thinking only of the warm bath that she would have before bed. Only that, and the warmth of Alma at one side and Lucy at the other, kept her going step by step. Grace had been asked to join the night staff as they were short of nurses after a softly spoken Irish nurse, who'd only been with them for four days, had died from the flu and two more had fallen ill. It pleased Emily to have a vision of Grace with a lamp, just like Florence Nightingale, her red hair shining as she tended to her patients like the guardian angel that she truly was.

As they filed into the nurses' residence, Sister Kelly was there to meet them, taking their cloth masks to send to the laundry for a boil wash. 'Well done, nurses,' she said as they trudged in through the door, their faces flushed and bearing the tell-tale red marks across nose and cheeks where the masks had left their imprint.

'Oh, Nurse Adams,' she called, seeing Alma drift by, 'please can you pass on our most grateful thanks to your aunt.' Emily saw Alma frown – clearly she had no idea why or what for. 'This afternoon a taxi cab pulled up outside – Miss Foster has sent boxes of cake and biscuits and bottles of wine for the nurses.'

'Has she?' Alma cracked a smile. 'How unexpected.'

'She sent a note, thanking the nurses for their sterling work and telling me not to let anybody know who the donor was, but I wanted to tell you – it really is a lovely gesture.'

'Yes, it is.'

'So, I've decided there will be a special supper this evening. I've pinned a poster to the noticeboard on each of the three floors to let everyone know. And I made sure that the night staff had some treats before they went on duty.'

'Well, thank you,' said Alma. 'Thank you very much.'

'No, don't thank me, this is all down to your aunt, and I will be writing to her to express our gratitude. In these dark times, we need every boost that we can get.'

The special supper went down a treat and brought some extra life back into the tired nurses. As they left the dining room they all took something with them – Emily chose wine and Lucy some cake and biscuits. 'Come on Ems,' whispered Lucy, 'Let's go back to my room and have a listen to the gramophone, like old times.'

'Excellent idea,' Emily said, leading the way with her half bottle of wine.

The scratchy needle on the portable wind-up gramophone instantly brought back every other happy occasion when Emily and Lucy had shared a 'dance in' as they called it. Lucy only had three records but they were all well-loved and after another few swigs of wine they were ready to go. Still in their uniforms they adopted their positions – gleaned from Sunday School socials and Lucy's dance classes. As the first crackles and the opening bars of 'When Irish Eyes are Smiling' started to play, Emily snorted with laughter seeing Lucy's serious expression – she could never remember if she was the man or the woman, or why, or who should be leading. Once Mr Fred Douglas started to sing, Lucy moved and Emily stumbled after her. There was so little space that all they could do was go round in a circle. They were both laughing now. 'Come on,' called Lucy, 'we need to catch the rhythm of the music.' Emily straightened up and held onto Lucy's hand and around her waist. They'd just got back into their stride when the needle stuck. Laughing uproariously now they both made a staccato movement in time with the repetitive scratch, scratch, before collapsing down on the bed.

Lucy went to lift the needle and pull the record up off the gramophone, wiping round it with a handkerchief before setting it back on the turntable. As the crackles started again, she came back to the bed with two pieces of cake. 'We'll just have a rest,' she said, 'And then we'll go for round two.'

As Mr Fred Douglas got into his stride , they were both singing along and once the cake was finished, they were up and dancing again. After Lucy replayed the record two more times, they settled on the bed finally. Emily lay back against Lucy's pillow, a trace of buttercream at the side of her mouth. 'That was fun,' she said, 'isn't it nice to do something different? I can't remember the last time we had such a laugh.'

'I know,' murmured Lucy, nestling her head on Emily's lap. 'This takes me back to our first few weeks together.'

Emily reached out a hand to stroke Lucy's hair. 'It's strange isn't it, but even though we've only known each other these last few years, it feels like we've grown up together.'

'Like sisters,' Lucy murmured, stifling a yawn.

'Yes, that's exactly what we are; that's what living and working together does…'

Emily dozed and then nodded herself awake, rousing Lucy who was gently snoring with a biscuit still grasped in her hand.

'Time for bed,' she groaned, wriggling off the bed and staggering to the door. 'Good night, Luce, sleep well.'

The next morning, Emily was putting the finishing touches to her hair when Lucy tapped on the door and came straight in. Her face looked pale and pinched set against her jet-black hair and she had grey smudges beneath her eyes, but she still managed a bright smile and helped Emily fix the last couple of hair pins to try and keep her thick locks in place. Once she was done, Lucy kissed her on the cheek and then started rooting in her pocket. 'Here, I saved this from last night,' she said, snapping a shortbread biscuit in half and passing the biggest portion to Emily.

Emily took it gratefully. 'Thanks, we need all the fuel we can get.'

As they filed downstairs, Alma slipped in beside them. She managed to still look sleek and beautiful in her uniform and, as always, she had a bright smile. Sister Kelly was standing at the door, handing each of them a clean mask and repeating the advice to keep their faces away from those who were coughing – which they all knew was impossible – to make sure that the mask stayed in position throughout the shift, and most of all to wash hands between patients. 'Please, nurses, do remember the words of our dearly departed Miss Nightingale: "The least carelessness in not washing your hands between one bad case and another… may cost a life."'

'Thank you, Sister,' said each nurse politely as she donned her mask. When there were enough clean supplies on the ward, they would also be issued with a white cotton theatre gown to wear over their uniforms. They all flitted around the ward in their whites, only identifiable by hair colour and eyes above the mask – like ghostly warriors in battle against an unseen enemy.

As they walked through the hospital corridor, Emily saw Dr Cantor scanning the ranks of nurses. She wondered if, for some reason, he might be looking for her. Immediately, she pushed the thought away. He *was* looking in her direction though… She then realised it was Alma whom he wanted to speak to. As her friend broke step to talk to him, Emily sighed and couldn't stop herself from glancing back to see them deep in conversation.

Lucy gave her arm a squeeze. 'They're both American, that's why they're always chatting.'

It made Emily feel even more irritated, knowing that Lucy had noticed her discomfort. 'I'm not bothered about that,' she said abruptly, feeling her cheeks start to flush, and then hastily continued, 'and, in fact, Dr Cantor is Canadian. So, strictly speaking, they're not both American. But you're right, they have something different about them. Not like me and you, hey, we're cut from the same cloth – me from Lancashire, you from Yorkshire.'

'Even if Yorkshire is better,' Lucy joked. But then, alarmingly, she started to cough and the two nurses in front twisted round, their eyes wide with concern.

'I'm fine, just a biscuit crumb,' croaked Lucy, clearing her throat and pulling a handkerchief from her pocket.

Emily's own chest felt tight, just that one bout of coughing had cut through everything else and exposed the deep worry that each had, that this horrible disease might eventually take a grip on them all. She needed to take a deep breath, in and out, to steady herself. Lucy was her best friend, what if something happened to her?

'I'm all right, stop fretting…'

Emily scrutinised Lucy's face, her colour was good, she didn't look sick.

As they reached the intersection of corridors where she went one way and Lucy went the other, Emily saw Lucy give her usual glance as if to say 'here goes' and with a smile, she murmured goodbye. But this now felt different to any other morning and Emily wanted to pull her back, give her a hug. She held her breath as she continued to walk, glancing back one more time, but Lucy was gone. Just as she started to tell herself not to be ridiculous, Alma caught her up, breathless, and the moment was forgotten. 'James was asking me if I've heard from my parents in Richmond, he hasn't had a letter from his family in ages and he's getting a bit worried.'

'Oh dear, do you think they're all right?' asked Emily, feeling relieved, then in the next breath caught by the gnawing concern that they all had, especially those who were far from home, that any of their families – be it in England, America or on Prince Edward Island – could be struck down by this deadly disease. And there was nothing that they would be able to do about it. This anxiety rested unspoken between them... it seemed that no one wanted to risk tempting fate by talking about some dreadful thing that might become a reality.

Alma gave a sigh but when she spoke her voice was determinedly upbeat. 'I think his family will be absolutely fine, the mail has probably just been delayed. I told him that I had a letter from my mom last week and all she was worried about was that the theatres and the restaurants were closed. I tried to perk him up – he can be a bit sombre at times – but then again his folks are a farming family and the community that they live in is so different from mine, so maybe he's right to be worried. I didn't say that to him of course.'

'No, of course not,' murmured Emily.

'Have you heard anything from your family?' Alma asked.

Emily was struck by shame – she'd been meaning to write for days but always found herself side-tracked or simply too exhausted. She hadn't heard from her family for a couple of weeks. 'Not recently, but I'm due a letter soon...' she stumbled out, vowing to make time to write this evening.

Grace made a beeline for them, looking dishevelled – no wonder really, by all accounts the night shifts were horrendous and they were always short-staffed. She pulled her mask down to speak. 'Emily, just to let you know, young Sid Wilkins has gone down with a fever, we've been tepid sponging him overnight to keep him cool and he hasn't developed a cough as yet, but I just wanted you to be aware… I know you've got a soft spot for him.'

'Oh what a shame, thanks for telling me.' Emily felt the growing emptiness inside her widen. 'I'll make sure to keep an eye on him. You get off the ward, hope you have a good sleep.'

'I'll try…' Grace's presence was usually reassuring but now, seeing how even she struggled with the work, it was unsettling.

An hour into the shift, Dr Cantor appeared at the top of the ward, glancing frantically at the nurses who were flitting up and down. *He must be looking for Alma again*, she thought. With all the nurses in white gowns today, it would be hard for him to spot her, so Emily pulled down her mask and called out to him, pointing across the ward to where Alma was helping a patient out of bed.

She saw him shake his head and he walked rapidly in her direction. 'I need you in theatre, immediately,' he said, as soon as he was close enough. 'We have an emergency admission, a flu case for Caesarean section. There is very little time. Go now – run. I'll speak to Sister.'

Emily took a breath, pulled up her mask and started to run, her heart thudding against her ribs. She'd heard that Theatre Sister was down with the flu, but other staff must be sick as well, otherwise James wouldn't be asking for her – she'd only worked with him that once. She had assisted with a Caesarean before though, thank goodness; they all did a stint on the lying-in ward as part of their training. As she ran, she tried to recall the instruments – the procedure was pretty basic from what she could remember. But what did fill her with dread was the inescapable fact that the chance of both mother and baby surviving the operation was slim – the bleeding during surgery was horrendous. She'd seen the baby that she'd help to deliver die in the arms of the anaesthetist.

Dr McKenzie was already in theatre and, thankfully, he had prepared a tray of steam-sterilised instruments. He glanced up and nodded as Emily headed past him to the sink to scrub her hands. She knew that the patient was coming as soon as she heard the rumble of a hospital trolley. The hairs on the back of her neck prickled. The woman was wheezing and fighting for breath. Drying her hands rapidly, Emily rushed to the trolley just as James bounded in through the door.

She was heartbroken by the scene: the poor woman's lips were blue and her face was mottled, she was opening and closing her mouth but hardly breathing. Beneath the sheet, the curve of her pregnant belly rose and fell with each ragged breath.

'Hello,' Emily said, forcing her voice to steady, 'I'm a nurse, my name is Emily, and I'm going to do everything I can to help you and your baby.'

The porter, his face drained of colour, steered the trolley towards the theatre table. Emily felt James by her side.

'I'm sure I felt the baby move when I was using a Pinard stethoscope to listen for the foetal heart. I couldn't find a heartbeat, but that might just be positional...' he said hurriedly. 'That's why we're doing this... there is a chance that the child might still be alive.'

'Let's get her on the table,' Dr McKenzie said, his voice business-like. 'On three, slide her across.'

'Do we know her name?' Emily asked. The porter was standing beside the theatre table with his head bowed. He looked up and when he spoke, his voice was shaky with emotion. 'She's called Rose, that was all she could tell us. I've never seen anything like this, not even when I was on the front line... men poisoned with gas fared better than this.' Trembling, he straightened up the trolley and wheeled it solemnly towards the door.

Switching her attention immediately back to her patient, she began to speak, keeping her voice steady. 'Rose, I promise you, we're going to do all we can to save your baby.'

The woman's breathing had slowed right down. Dr McKenzie had the anaesthetic mask in his hand and the chloroform stood ready, but he looked over the table to James and suggested, 'It will pass through to the foetus… I don't want to risk any more compromise to the unborn child. What do you think?'

Scalpel already in his hand, James paused, before replying, 'I agree, let's try without, but if there's the slightest hint of her being aware, we'll use it straight away.' The anaesthetist nodded in agreement.

Emily felt a surge of energy pulse through her body and she took a breath to increase her focus.

'We need to move fast,' James said as he swept a vertical incision right down the woman's abdomen. There was no glimmer of a reaction from Rose as she took her last few breaths. James cut quickly through the layers as Emily passed swabs. When he punctured the uterus, a gush of amniotic fluid spurted out. This was visceral work and he needed both hands to deliver the baby's head, to reach inside the woman's body and grapple to release the infant. Once the head was out, the shoulders quickly followed, blood pouring to the floor.

Emily glanced frantically at McKenzie, who just shook his head and murmured, 'She's already gone.' Emily gritted her teeth as James held the baby up, away from the mother's body, the cord dangling down. She saw that it was a boy and she took him, his limp body slippery in her hands, so that James could cut the cord. She bit back a sob as James set the child free from his mother and then she was walking quickly with him held against her body, to a table that had been prepared with a soft towel and some basic equipment. She laid the baby down – there was still no sign of life. James was straight there, by her side, and he started rubbing the baby's body, his skin was dark blue against the white towel.

'Use this to clear his nose and mouth,' Emily ordered, passing him a bulb syringe. James depressed the rubber bulb and pushed the tube into the child's mouth, sucking out the mucus, once, twice, three times. There was still no glimmer of life and James was starting to shake his head, ready to give up. A surge of what felt like rage rose up in Emily and she took the baby from James, turning him over onto his tummy, using the towel again to rub his small, helpless back. Still there was nothing.

James stepped back.

'I'm not giving up, not yet,' warned Emily, rubbing more vigorously with the towel. She was desperate now and acting on no more than instinct. She turned the baby over, pulling down her mask and placing her lips over the child's nose and mouth and steadily breathing out. She gave his body another rub and then again she breathed, a little harder this time, so that she could feel the child's chest rising. Again, she gave another breath, and another, and then she rolled the baby onto his side to rub him with the towel before grabbing the bulb syringe to suck out one more time. She barely realised she was sobbing now as she covered his nose and mouth and breathed one more time. Suddenly, she felt a tiny movement, a whisper of breath like a butterfly wing.

'I've got something!' she called, giving another breath. The child moved an arm and then a leg. With another breath, he gave a weak cry, like a sickly kitten. James gasped with delight and he was rubbing the baby's body too, almost jubilant. She stood back for a moment, catching her breath; she could have whooped with joy. Then, she glanced at the shrouded figure of the baby's mother on the table, blood seeping through the sheet that McKenzie had draped over her. Pulling her mask up, she approached the body and stroked back the woman's hair. 'Your baby is alive, Rose, you have a boy and he is alive.'

'Emily, I want you to stay with the baby, wrap him up, keep him warm, I need to go and find one of the nurses on the lying-in ward.'

'Yes, of course,' she replied to James.

She took the baby in her arms. He was so tiny – he must have been some weeks premature – and had tufts of hair plastered down on his head. He was breathing independently but his breath was shallow. It made her heart ache even more for the tiny scrap of life. She cradled him, rocking him in her arms, seeing his dark eyes blinking at her. She was talking to him, saying anything that came into her head, terrified that he would stop breathing, and that by the time James came back they would be fighting to save his life again.

She could hear McKenzie attending to the dead mother on the theatre table. He was washing her face and hands and cleaning up the wound, packing her abdomen to absorb some of the blood. Emily took the baby over to the head of the table, wanting to make sure that he was close to his mother, just for a final few moments.

McKenzie looked up. 'She didn't stand any chance of survival. I've never seen anything like this pandemic… It's like no other flu.'

'What is it? Have we any idea?' she asked.

McKenzie narrowed his eyes, considering for a moment. 'A doctor I know has been culturing sputum under the microscope and he's seeing the same kind of bacteria that you'd expect in pneumonia… and some are saying that's it, that's the cause, so let's start on a vaccine. But how can it be? They're missing something, they have to be, whatever this is, it's completely new.'

'Maybe there is a microbe there, but it's far too small to be seen by a microscope?' Emily offered as the baby gently squirmed against her body.

McKenzie shook his head. 'You might be right, but all I know is that whatever it is, it's filling patients' lungs with so much fluid that they're drowning. We need more time to study it, but it's ripping through every city in the world… there is no time.' She heard him sigh heavily and then he pulled out a pencil and a piece of paper from his pocket and began to write out the scant detail of their patient: 'Rose' and the date and time of her death. He pinned the note to her dress and then covered her body with a fresh white sheet, ready for removal to the mortuary. He glanced up to Emily. 'We're not giving up on this though, we have to keep going.'

The door flew open and James came in, carrying a bundle of items for the newborn: a baby's nightie, a knitted hat, a napkin and two cot blankets. He handed them over and Emily laid the baby down so that she could dress him – one thing that she remembered about premature babies was how important it was to keep them warm. If Rose had lived, they would have given her the baby to nurse next to her skin.

As she was working, James was talking rapidly by her side. 'I've spoken to Nurse Berry on the lying-in ward and we're going to try something new. They've recently acquired something called an incubator – it's basically a heated glass box with a hatched side for sickly and premature babies. They've only used it a couple of times but Nurse Berry said they've had some measure of success and she's keen to try. If we take the baby up there, she said she'd supervise it herself.'

'That's good…' But a knot of anxiety had already formed in Emily's stomach. As she'd been dressing the baby, she'd noted that his colour had become dusky and she could see that his breathing still wasn't quite right; the poor little soul would most likely die.

She walked beside James, carrying the baby, as they made their way to the lying-in ward. Nurse Agatha Berry greeted them as they entered the side ward where she was busy making her preparations. A rosy-cheeked woman with round, wire-rimmed glasses and frizzy, steel-grey hair, she was the mainstay of baby care at the Infirmary. She'd worked at the hospital ever since it opened and if anyone was going to save Rose's baby, it was Nurse Berry.

'Now then, let's have a look at the little fella,' she said, holding out her arms for the baby. 'Ah, yes, he is a bit underdone isn't he? I'd say about three or four weeks premature. And we have the added complication that his mother was infected with the Spanish flu – as yet I've not heard of any cases of the babies surviving, but that doesn't mean there can't be a first. And from what we've been told it sounds like the woman took ill and died very quickly so there wasn't as much time for the child to suffer the consequences of her illness, so that might be in his favour…' All the time that she was talking, she had the baby on her knee and she was examining him. 'First things first, let's get him warmed up.' She swaddled him in one of the blankets, opened up the side of the glass incubator and placed him on a thick pad and folded sheet in the middle of the glass box. When she closed the door, Emily couldn't help but feel a pang of emotion– the baby looked so tiny and so alone in there.

'Don't be worrying,' Nurse Berry reassured, 'I'm going to stay right here by his side and when he's ready I'll try him with a few drops of milk. So, as far as we know, there's no sign of any family?' she asked, passing a clean cotton swab for James to use as a handkerchief, having noticed his glassy eyes.

Emily stepped in to answer, 'That's right, the woman came in alone, all we know is that she was called Rose.'

'Well, I always think that it's important to give a name to the babies whose mothers have died, the ones who might end up being orphans. What do you think? What would be a good name for him?'

Emily and James looked at each other, bewildered for a moment. His voice was husky when he spoke, 'How about Jacob? My father died last year and he was a Jacob.'

'That's a good name,' said Nurse Berry, blinking as she looked through the glass of the incubator to the baby. 'It's strong, he'll need that.'

*

As they walked back together along the corridor, Emily began to feel a bit light-headed. She fished in her pocket, hoping that by accident she might have left half a biscuit in there, but no luck. She felt stifled by the mask so she pulled it down and took in a few good breaths of air. She saw James do the same.

'It gets a bit much, doesn't it, always being muffled behind a cloth mask?' It was so refreshing to see him smile – she realised just how much she missed seeing people's faces.

When she smiled back at him, it felt freeing.

Some of the windows along the corridor had been left open to let the air in. The hospital staff had been trained under the guiding philosophy of Florence Nightingale – they all knew the importance of strict hygiene and ventilation. This hospital, like many others, had been designed specifically to keep the air moving through. It could get cold and draughty, but it kept down the rate of infection. Emily walked to the window and James followed. As they both breathed in and out, she had the sensation that they were breathing as one, in time with each other. She could have stayed there for ever, but on the ward they'd all still be running around like crazy, without any chance of a break. And she still hadn't managed to see Sid – she needed to double-check that they were up to date with his treatment.

She turned to James and opened her mouth to speak but the moment was broken by the sound of church bells. The bells were ringing all at once, pealing out, loud and clear. A clean and joyful sound. This wasn't a regular marking of the time. Down below, they could hear the sounds of running feet and voices shouting.

Emily craned her neck to see what was going on. 'What the heck is that?' she said, still puzzled. The sound of a commotion and then a bedraggled cheer from one of the wards down the corridor made them glance at each other before the realisation started to dawn.

'Is that what I think it might be?' Emily grinned, grabbing James by the arm and almost jumping up and down on the spot.

'The war's over!' called one of the porters, emitting an exultant cheer as he ran past, and then turned to shout back in their direction. 'It's bloody well over!'

James grabbed her, both arms around her, and he lifted her up off the ground. They were both laughing, and in that split second when he put her back down, he looked straight at her, his eyes burning. She was sure that he was going to kiss her. She gazed at him expectantly, her body tingling. Then, she felt a stab of realisation and, instinctively, she was stepping back. She had no choice. Knowing that Lewis would be sharing this same moment somewhere in France – stuck God knows where, desperate to get home – she couldn't let this happen.

Seeing the disappointment in James's eyes, she tried to laugh it off, pretend she hadn't noticed the way that he'd been looking at her. But her body refused to deny it – and she knew that she had wanted to kiss him, right there in the corridor; she'd wanted to throw her arms around him and press her body tight against him.

'The war is over!' she repeated, trying to make her voice light. She pulled her mask back up and turned away, leaving James in the corridor, gazing after her. As she walked, she made herself think about Lewis. She tried to picture his face but she couldn't get an image of him; all she could remember was the dullness of his eyes the last time he'd been home on leave. Even his voice seemed to have slipped away. He would be back soon… and then what? That's when it hit her. She knew what he would be expecting – he would be asking for them to be married and then she would become a wife and have to leave London, leave the work that she loved. And she wasn't ready to give it all up, not yet.

CHAPTER 7

Dunkirk, France

November 11, 1918

Lewis could hear church bells ringing, then loud voices, too, and the sound of cheering. Was he getting married? He couldn't remember…Then he caught the sound of a child's voice, as if a little girl was standing beside his bed, but his eyes were heavy, so heavy that he couldn't open them properly. His heart was pounding and he could feel the hot stickiness of his body, there was a blanket over him, it was weighing him down.

He tried to raise himself up on the bed but he could barely lift his head off the pillow. 'Help, help me,' he croaked, his voice weak and his tongue sticking to the roof of his mouth.

'You're all right,' came a soft voice above him.

The light hurt as he opened his eyes and all he could see was bright white. He blinked, his eyelids were scratchy and making his eyes water. When he opened his eyes again, he could make out the shape of a face swimming into view. Blinking again, his vision cleared enough to see it was a pale beautiful face framed by a white veil. *Oh Christ*, he thought, *this is an angel, I must be dead after all.*

'Do you want a drink of water, Sergeant Dupree?' asked the angel, her voice was clear and beautifully accented.

He tried to say 'yes', but his voice stuck somewhere in his throat.

She offered him some sips from a spouted cup. The water was cool and tasted so refreshing he drank greedily, feeling it spill down his chin. 'More,' he croaked, desperate now, not knowing if there could be enough water to properly quench his thirst. In the moment he heard the earthly clink of a glass jug on the spouted cup that had fed him, he realised that he was alive.

'Where am I?' he croaked, after the angel had told him that he'd had enough water for now. His voice was starting to clear a little.

The angel wiped his mouth with a soft cloth. 'You are in a hospital on the French coast, at Dunkirk.'

'What's wrong with me? Have I been hit?'

'No, no, you have the influenza, Sergeant Dupree.'

He seemed to be grasping it now; he had some memory of being in a hospital tent and then being jolted in an ambulance and put on a train with other fellas, all coughing their guts up. *Yes, that's right, that was it.*

There was more cheering again, loud, hurting his head.

He frowned, tried to raise himself up in bed.

'They are celebrating because the war is over,' said the nurse, smiling now. 'We will all be going home soon.'

Lewis felt a surge of elation, he wanted to laugh and shout with joy but it just set him off coughing. After he'd brought up the phlegm and spat it into a bowl offered by the nurse, he felt his chest sear with pain.

'There, there.' She wiped his face and then his mouth with a soothing damp cloth.

He started to cry, an overwhelming sorrow rising from deep inside. He knew that if he didn't let it out, it could kill him.

The nurse passed him a clean white handkerchief. 'There, there, Sergeant Dupree, just let it go.'

He buried his face in the clean cloth, starting to get back some control. And then with a jolt, he realised just how sick he had become. It was all so unexpected; he'd been fighting this goddamned war for four years and he'd survived every bit of it, but now he'd just woken up in hospital and he hadn't even been shot or gassed. He tried to laugh at the ridiculousness of it all, but found himself hacking with a cough.

Once the paroxysm of coughing subsided, he rolled onto his side. His chest was raw, he had never felt so ill in his whole life. He knew that he had to get out of here, he'd survived years of shelling in the trenches; he couldn't be beaten by this, not now.

CHAPTER 8

St Marylebone Infirmary, London

November 11, 1918

That evening as the nurses walked back from the wards there was a buzz of excitement. News of the armistice had ricocheted through the hospital, and even though they were exhausted from nursing so many flu cases all day long, there were cackles of laughter and whispers of excitement. At the sound of fireworks going off outside, they started to cheer and crowd by the windows to watch the display. Some of the nurses were planning to go out and join in the celebrations; others just wanted to stay home and rejoice away from the hustle and bustle. Emily would have loved to have run out and danced in the street – it had been bubbling inside of her all day, and Alma was up for it too, her eyes now extra bright with excitement.

But Emily simply couldn't – Lucy had come off the ward looking awful. Her face was white and her eyes were swollen and she could hardly hold her head up. As soon as Emily had rested the back of her hand against Lucy's forehead, she knew that her friend was burning up with a terrible fever.

'Come on, Luce,' Emily said holding her up, making her voice light but feeling dread grip her heart. 'Let's get you back and then we can tuck you up in bed.' Alma came round to the other side and as they assisted Lucy along the corridor, they exchanged a horrified glance. They were both thinking the worst: Lucy had the flu.

As soon as Sister Kelly saw them approaching, she walked out to meet them, her face knotted with concern.

'Well now, Nurse Bennett,' she said calmly, 'you do seem to be looking a bit under the weather this evening… I think it would be a good idea if you went straight to the nurses' sick bay, just so that we can check you over.'

'Please don't worry about me,' Lucy was trying to say, but there was a creak in her voice and her head was drooping.

'It might be a good idea,' Emily urged, 'so that we can make sure that you're comfortable. Come on, Luce. I'll stay with you.'

'Don't you want to go out and celebrate?'

'Well I was thinking about it but, do you know what, I'm dog-tired – I don't want to be going out, I'll stay with you instead.'

'But it's the biggest night of the century…' Lucy's voice tailed off and Emily felt her friend's legs start to sag.

Between Alma and Emily, they managed to prop her up and walk her the short distance to the sick bay.

Sister Kelly hovered in the background as they helped Lucy change into a hospital nightdress and settled her between the crisp, clean sheets of the iron-framed bed. 'Make sure she has these two aspirin,' she said, her voice tinged with emotion, 'and I'll go and get the doctor. Nurse Adams, please go to the kitchen for a full jug of water.'

Alma was already bustling out of the door. Emily would start getting as much fluid as she could inside Lucy as soon as she returned.

'I'm so sorry,' Lucy croaked, one big tear running down her cheek. 'I don't want to be a nuisance.'

Emily grabbed Lucy's hand, fighting to keep her own tears at bay. 'Don't be daft, don't forget you stayed with me when I went down with that fever in the spring, you never left my side all night.'

'I'd forgotten about that… And you got better… didn't you?' Her voice was almost a whisper now as she was drifting off to sleep.

Emily put a hand to her mouth to hold back the sobs but they couldn't be kept in. How could Lucy have become so poorly, so quickly? As she lay now in the hospital bed, her face starting to pour with sweat and her breath rasping in her chest, she looked like she was dying. Emily sobbed again, muffling it with her hand, forcing herself to be quiet. She grabbed a handful of the bed sheet and squeezed it so tight it made her hand hurt. Her body was rigid with fear.

'Here's the water,' Alma's quiet voice made her turn. Alma gasped and reached out, wrapping Emily in her arms. 'Are you all right?' she said. 'You need to go outside, have a walk around, give yourself some time to get yourself together.'

As Alma helped Emily towards the door, Emily looked back, incredulous, to Lucy lying in the bed. She didn't want to leave her best friend, but she knew that Alma was right. 'I'll make sure she has the aspirin and a good drink of water,' Alma said quietly. 'You have to take a break…'

Emily nodded, unable to speak.

As soon as Emily was out through the door of the nurses' home, the night air struck cold on her face. She drew in a sharp breath and started to walk fast. Two nurses returning late from the ward, chatting excitedly, glanced at her with concern, but she just kept going. Once she was far enough away, she knew that she needed to let it out, but she had to find an open space.

She glanced up to the dark sky, feeling like she could howl with pain but she made herself keep walking towards the open land at the back of the hospital, where the tennis courts that the nurses had used before the war now stood empty and overgrown with weeds. It was a forlorn, forgotten place but Emily knew that it was just the right spot for her to be. As soon as she reached the abandoned tennis court, she walked up to the wire mesh and clung to it, feeling the wire digging into her fingers. She finally allowed herself to cry, to just let it go.

When the worst of it was over, she gazed up to the sky again, breathing in great lungfuls of air. Anxious now about being away from Lucy's bedside, Emily forced herself to straighten up. She needed to be fully together and razor sharp, these early hours were crucial for Lucy.

She focussed on a single bright star in the sky, staring at it so hard it made her eyes hurt. 'Right, come on,' she said out loud to herself, 'you've got work to do.'

Just as she turned, she saw a black shape approaching.

'Sorry,' a voice said – a North American voice. She could see his face as he came up close, it was James. 'Sorry to startle you,' he said, 'there isn't usually anyone else out here... I often come, just to get some air. I grew up on an island of green fields and trees, sometimes I find the city—'

'That's alright, I was just going back anyway.'

'Emily?' he said, leaning in to look closer. 'Emily, are you OK?'

The genuine concern in his voice brought her to the brink of tears again. She gulped in some more air and balled her hands into a tight fist. 'Yes,' she said firmly. 'It's just that my best friend, she looks very poorly, we're sure that she has the Spanish flu.'

'I'm sorry to hear that... Do you want me to examine her?'

She was already shaking her head. 'No, Sister Kelly has already gone for a doctor – Dr Marsden usually sees the nurses.'

'Well if you need anything at all, just let me know. I live on the ground floor of the doctor's residence.'

'I will, and... thank you,' she said. 'I should get going, Alma's with her but I don't want to be away for too long.'

'Of course. What a day you've had, with our emergency delivery and the baby and now this...' He took a step closer.

'I hope your friend improves,' he said, and then as if it was the most natural thing in the world, he reached out and put his arms around her, pulling her close. She could feel his cheek against her hair, the warmth of him. Given the choice, she would have rested there with her head against his chest for ever. It felt like the safest place in the world.

'I'd best be off,' she murmured, taking a step back as he slowly released her.

He cleared his throat. 'Yes of course.'

'I'll see you tomorrow,' she said quietly. 'Thank you...'

As she walked towards the nurses' home, she was already thinking through what she needed to do for Lucy – plenty of fluids, tepid-sponging, make sure she was sitting upright in bed, hourly pulse and temperature. And she'd make sure that the window was open a notch, get the air circulating... They'd need the fire lit as well, and maybe a steam kettle would help her breathing.

As she approached the sick bay, she heard the harsh bark of a cough and it sent a stab of anxiety through her. Opening the door, she was horrified to see Lucy fighting for breath. Alma was clinging to her, trying to keep her calm, but she was struggling.

'The doctor came with Sister Kelly, he didn't stay long and he confirmed our worst thoughts. They've given her an injection of strychnine to try and stimulate her, but then she started like this,' Alma gasped, out of breath herself.

'I'll take her... Lucy, listen to me, you need to calm down.'

'Don't let me die!' Lucy cried. 'Please don't let me die.'

'I won't,' Emily said firmly, taking the spouted cup and telling Lucy to drink as much as she could. 'Pass me two pillows off the other bed,' she instructed Alma, who was standing by, rigid.

Alma helped Emily arrange them so that Lucy was sitting upright and her breathing improved instantly. 'That's much better, isn't it,' Alma sighed out. 'Now what else do you want me to do?'

Emily grabbed Alma's hand and looked her in the eye. 'Now that we've got her in a better position, I can manage this. And there's only one thing that I want you to do right now – I want you to go out into the city and celebrate for us. Sister Kelly will be back soon and we can manage between us, someone needs to go out and mark the end of this bloody awful war.'

'No, I couldn't, not with—'

'You have to,' Emily insisted. 'Do this for me and for Lucy. Now go – go!'

'It just doesn't feel right...' Alma said, frowning.

'Lucy's been going on and on about celebrating the end of the war, every single day she's told me what a good time we'll have. She would want you to go, she even told *me* to go out earlier...'

'Are you sure?' murmured Alma.

Emily nodded fiercely. It felt like absolutely the right thing to do and at least they'd have some stories to tell Lucy when she was feeling better. And she knew that if Lucy came round and saw them both sitting by the bed, she would definitely think the worst, and it would frighten her. Alma gave Emily a hug before she left and took one last glance back from the door. Once Emily was alone with Lucy, she began to feel more relaxed, more in charge.

Sister Kelly came bustling in with a steam kettle in her hand. The fire had already been lit but there was no warmth from it yet. With the window open, the room was cool and that was good – they needed to get Lucy's fever down. Sister checked that everything was to hand and then she came up close and stroked Lucy's arm. Emily could hear Sister whispering some words under her breath; she couldn't quite catch them but it sounded like a prayer. When Sister turned, she spoke clearly. 'I know you'll want to sit with her, Nurse Burdon, so I'll make sure that Sister Montgomery knows that you might not be on the ward in the morning. And I'll send a telegram to Lucy's family first thing tomorrow.'

Emily drew in a breath, as if she was going to say something, but no words came.

Sister reached out a hand to her. 'I'm going to be just next door all night and I'll come in every hour. Shout out if you need anything. I'll bring in one of the armchairs from my sitting room so that you'll be more comfortable and I'll have some supper sent and… and over there,' she pointed to a pile of linen on top of a chest of drawers, 'we have a supply of gowns and masks. We need to keep up professional standards, especially when we're nursing our own.'

During the early part of the night, there was little time to sit in the chair. Lucy was burning up with fever and she needed almost constant sponging with cool water. When the coughing fits came, Emily would hold her arm around Lucy's shoulders, steadying her, seeing her through the worst of it. It seemed like they had only minutes to rest in between and then it was back again and even with another dose of aspirin there was no settling down as the infection raged through Lucy's body.

At around two in the morning, after Lucy had come through yet another bout of coughing, Emily noticed a difference in her. Sister had helped and they'd sponged her down, changed her nightgown and the bed sheets, which were saturated with sweat and they'd stacked the pillows so that she was sat up high in the bed. Lucy had opened her eyes and smiled at them, apologising for being a nuisance. She looked fragile against the pillow, her dark eyes wide. Emily had pulled down her mask and kissed her on the forehead, squeezed her hand, told her that she loved her. Lucy had settled after that, it seemed like she was sleeping and Emily had been able to rest back in the armchair beside the warm flicker of the fire and close her eyes.

*

Emily woke with a start to the sound of fireworks exploding somewhere out in the city – the celebrations were still going on. At some point earlier, Alma had come back, buzzing with excitement, alive with the detail of it all – the singing and dancing in the street, the press of bodies. She'd had a drink for each of them and she'd walked past the statue of Florence Nightingale and seen a drunken soldier who'd shimmied up and put an arm around her, shouting, *God bless good old Florence, we couldn't have done it without her!* and then he'd slipped and fallen with a crash onto the ground. Thankfully he wasn't badly hurt and he was soon up and limping away; imagine if he'd broken a leg and ended up as one of their patients? It made Emily smile, thinking about it, she knew that it would be a good story to tell Lucy. Alma had tried to insist that she stay but Emily had been clear – the wards were so busy and they were so short-staffed, one of them had to be fit and able to go to work in the morning.

Emily got up to check on Lucy, who was still sleeping and looked comfortable, nestled against the white pillows. She didn't want to disturb her for a drink just yet, best to let her sleep whilst she could. She put some more coal on the fire and went back to the armchair – she must have fallen asleep again because the next thing she shot up when she heard a sudden sound from the bed. Lucy was hacking and bringing up frothy sputum.

'Spit it out,' Emily yelled, with a cloth and a bowl ready.

It was horrifying to hear the rattle of her friend's chest – like a death rattle. Emily gritted her teeth and she checked on Lucy's colour. Her lips and the tips of her fingers were pink – they were still on the right side of things.

Suddenly, her friend was struggling to push herself up and out of bed. Emily had no choice but to let her go. Lucy wanted to stand. She wheezed on every breath, then a heaving, harsh cough took her whole body and she spat out again – this time, there was a tinge of blood. Emily had seen this happen – when the disease progressed…

Sister Kelly was in through the door again, her voice breaking. 'The poor girl. Can we get her back into bed?'

'I've tried, she just doesn't want to lie down.'

Lucy was looking around frantically, her eyes wild. 'No, no!' she was shouting.

'She wants to stand up,' said Emily, holding onto Lucy.

'Where's Emily? I want Emily,' Lucy croaked.

Emily wrenched down her mask so that she could see her face. 'I'm here, Luce, I'm here.'

'Help me…' Her eyes were terrified as she clutched at Emily.

Emily swallowed hard and took Lucy's weight, propping her against the wall next to the bed head. Seeing her best friend like this, Emily started to break inside.

Sister Kelly put an arm around her shoulders. 'Let me take over, Nurse Burdon…'

Just the thought of walking away spurred Emily on. 'No, no,' she insisted, her voice choking on a sob.

Sister stepped back, saying something about getting the doctor back in.

'No, it'll just panic her even more, we can manage this.'

Sister wiped a hand over her face and then she nodded. Both of them knew that there was no more that anyone could do.

Another bout of coughing shook Lucy's body and a metallic smell exuded from her mouth. Her hair was coming undone, falling down in straggles across her fevered face. Emily reached for a damp flannel, wiping her friend's face, brushing back her hair, desperate to soothe her.

At last, Emily managed to get her to settle in the armchair. Lucy leant back in the chair and closed her eyes; it looked like she was calming at last. Momentarily, she opened her eyes, looked straight at Emily and smiled, a wobbly lop-sided smile, then she reached out.

Emily squeezed her hand, smiling back through gritted teeth and then speaking softly, 'I love you Luce, I'm here, I won't leave you'.

Lucy rested her head back against the chair and as she heaved out a sigh, her body relaxed. Emily saw her take another breath, clearer this time, and then she sighed again. For a moment, Emily thought that Lucy's breathing had settled. Then, she looked closer, and it was like a knife going through – Lucy's lips were dusky and her face was darkening. When she picked up her hand, her fingertips were dark blue.

As Emily clung to her hand, Lucy's chest rose for one final breath.

She felt something tilt and slip sideways. Lucy was completely still, her eyes black and unblinking.

Sister's arm was around her shoulders but Emily was shouting out now, 'No, no, no!'

'Hush now, hush,' Sister said, her voice ragged with emotion. 'There is absolutely nothing more that you could have done for your friend.'

CHAPTER 9

Time had stretched away slowly, agonisingly, since the moment Lucy had taken her last breath in the early hours of the morning.

Emily was sitting by the bed, snatches of what had passed running through her mind. The reality weighed her down. Lucy, who had been so vital, so full of life, lay so still on the bed, beneath a perfect white sheet. Sister Kelly had washed her body and combed her hair back neatly. Lucy never had tidy hair, everybody knew her with it always falling out from beneath her cap. She'd always been pale but her face was as white as her shroud now, and that solemn expression wasn't Lucy either – she had always been laughing. This effigy that lay on the bed with cool hands and blue lips was some travesty of the lovely girl that Emily had met on that first day of their training, when they had been two shy country girls wondering what the heck they'd got themselves into. They'd soon blossomed though – no nurse could be shy for long, not when there were patients to look after.

Don't let me die, Lucy had pleaded. Emily had promised and she had failed miserably. Agitated now, she jumped up knowing that if she didn't move she might rip down the curtains that shut out the light. 'I have to go, I'm sorry Luce,' she said, pulling off her white gown and letting it fall to the floor, running from the room with tears pouring once more down her cheeks.

Emily knew that she'd have to face people – all the nurses knew Lucy, especially their set of probationers. But she couldn't bear it, not yet. Bursting out through the main door, into the early morning light, the cold air hit her. This was the day they were meant to be joyous. The war was over. Instead, they would all be grieving and Sister Kelly was sending a devastating telegram to Lucy's family in Yorkshire, telling them that she had died bravely in the line of duty. None of this felt real, but Emily knew that she had to make it real.

Wiping her eyes with the flat of her hand she started to run, following the same path round to the back of the hospital that she'd taken last night. She didn't slow her pace until she was out of breath and then she forced herself to keep on walking. Somehow, it was no surprise to see James there again; it felt as if he was waiting for her. As soon as he glanced up and saw her approaching, his face showed that he understood.

She stood breathless in front of him.

'I'm so sorry,' he said. Seeing his unhappy face, something snapped inside of her and all she could feel was pure anger. It blazed out of her, 'Sorry?' she shouted. 'That can't be the right word, can it? Lucy was a beautiful young woman with the rest of her life before her, she hadn't even had a boyfriend… and now she is gone, just like that, and you're *sorry?*'

She saw him reel back, and then understanding started to dawn. He didn't say a word, he stepped forward and reached out an arm to her. Emily felt the ache in her chest spread until it surged out through her mouth in a gasping, sobbing agony. James didn't hesitate. He gathered her in his arms and she sobbed and sobbed against him. He stood for as long as it took, and after the worst of it had passed, he let go of her with one arm so that he could pull a clean, white handkerchief out of his pocket.

'Thank you,' she said, wiping her eyes. 'And I'm sorry for shouting at you like that.'

'Sorry isn't a word that we should be using,' he said, offering a tentative smile. 'And you've every right to rant and rave all you want. Come and find me anytime if you need to do it some more, I can take it… I sort of understand, you see, because when I was young my best friend died. We were both involved in an accident – he fell off the barn roof and I jumped down to try and save him. That's how I ended up with this limp. So I do know what you're going through right now.'

She was nodding. 'I feel like I'm just at the start of something, I've seen many people grieving… we do, don't we, in our line of work?'

He gave a wan smile. 'Yes, that's true, and I don't know if this works or not, but I do wonder sometimes if seeing all the losses here day by day, especially now with this flu, somehow seasons us, makes us better prepared. I'm not saying anyone gets used to death, but right now I'm probably seeing more dead bodies than I ever would have if they'd ignored my bad leg and let me join the army to fight on the front line.'

'No number of patients dying could prepare me for this… I cried for Rose yesterday, but there was a boundary to that, there has to be, otherwise we'd never be able to carry on and treat other patients. But this, well, Lucy and I started out together on our first day of training… We clicked straight away.'

'Was she the one who couldn't stop giggling when I saw you in the corridor on my first day?'

'Yes, that was Lucy… We were always together.'

'You're right, it is hard to lose one of our own – when you live and work beside someone, you become close. True friends. If I'd gone to war with the others, then I would have understood properly how it feels to lose a comrade, someone I'd fought alongside, that kind of thing.'

'Were you disappointed that you couldn't join up?'

'Yes, I was. I mean, all young men want to do their bit, prove themselves, but my leg was simply too damaged. It's improved since, but back then I sometimes needed a crutch to walk. And it just made me more frustrated to see my mother and father's relief… That's why I came to England to help out in the hospitals that were depleted of medical staff – first at St Thomas's and now, here, at the St Marylebone.'

'Well, I hope by now you're feeling that you've done your bit.'

'Yes, I truly am.'

'What time is it?' she said, as if surfacing from a trance. 'I need to get back, I should be getting ready for the ward.'

'No, no,' he was saying, shaking his head, 'you're not going anywhere today except your bed. You've been up all night and your friend has just died.'

She felt the weight hit her again and her shoulders slumped. 'Point taken. I think I remember Sister Kelly saying she'd spoken to Sister Montgomery. I might just go up and see baby Jacob, though.'

'You can if you want but don't stay long and don't get involved, doctor's orders. I've already been in there and I can report that the little fella is holding his own. He still isn't breathing all that well but he's taking some drops of milk and Nurse Berry is ever hopeful.'

Emily tried to smile but she was starting to feel a bit light-headed. 'That's good then, maybe I will leave it till tomorrow.'

She set off walking but lurched to the side as her legs felt weak.

He rushed to her aid. 'I know you might have an objection to me helping and if you start snarling at me I might run away, but I think that you could do with some assistance – you look fit to drop.'

'My legs are all wobbly,' she said faintly, 'so that would probably be a good idea… And I promise not to bite.'

She took his arm and they walked slowly. As they were approaching the door to the nurses' home, Alma walked out, her face tear-stained. She ran to Emily. 'There you are!' She grabbed hold of Emily and gave a quick glance to James to say thank you as she led her friend away.

'I don't know if I can go back in there…' Emily said, shaking her head.

'That's perfectly fine,' Alma replied. 'All of the nurses are gathered in the entrance hall and Sister Kelly wants to say some words to bring everybody together for a few minutes.

Emily still wasn't sure, she felt so exhausted and wrung out she just wanted to turn and walk away, but as soon as they came in through the door, she saw the nurses look to her, some of them crying. Their love for Lucy was obvious – and in that moment, she felt it envelop her.

Sister was standing at the front of the group and began, 'We all knew Lucy Bennett – she was one of the most enthusiastic probationers that I have ever had the privilege to work with. From her early days on the wards she embraced the challenge of nursing the sick and her patients always came first. She would do everything in her power to provide the best possible care…

'We all know the risks of doing the work that we do, I wouldn't like to give a number to the nurses I've known who have died from diseases that they caught in the line of duty, but what we are seeing now, in this city, is on another scale. Lucy is the second nurse from the St Marylebone to die from this terrible flu and many more are sick…

'Our Nurse Bennett showed immense courage, she was a shining light on the wards. I hope that we can maintain the spirit that she showed and continue with our work, we all know that is exactly what she would have wanted. Now let's stand together in a moment's silence…'

The nurses breathed as one, some with heads bowed, others with tears streaming down their faces. Emily felt the dull throb of pain in her chest expand and wrap itself around her heart.

When Sister raised her head and murmured a few more words, the nurses started to wipe their eyes and rouse themselves. They all knew that the patients were waiting – the work had to go on.

Sister stood quietly at the door, handing out masks. Seeing them all leave, Emily felt like she should go to work – if she engaged with the patients it would help to ease her and they were so short-staffed after all.

'Don't even think about it, Nurse Burdon,' said Sister Kelly. 'You have been awake all night and you've been through so much… You need to go and take your rest. We can't risk another nurse getting sick.'

'She's right,' Alma encouraged. 'Don't worry I'll make sure to check on Sid Wilkins for you…'

It seemed that Emily had no choice but to agree. Glancing down to the apron that she had been wearing since yesterday, she pulled it off and handed it to Sister. As she walked slowly up the stairs, she could still hear Lucy's voice as she chattered on and on, her hearty laughter bubbling and rising right up to the rafters of the high ceiling.

CHAPTER 10

Emily slept fitfully throughout the rest of the day and then the night. Lying in her bed, fully awake now, she was yearning for the pale November light to start showing through the window. She hadn't drawn the curtains – it made her think of Lucy lying so still on the bed in that room. Her head felt heavy, muzzy, as if she'd also been ill and she was just starting to make a shaky recovery. She curled up on her side – feeling the now familiar lump in her throat, she knew that she had to have another cry or she wouldn't be able to get herself up and ready for work.

As Emily dressed, Alma appeared through the door. 'We need to talk.' Emily stood in shock. Just a simple tap on the door had made her instantly forget and think it was Lucy – she would always come breezing in, their routine every morning before work.

'Are you OK?' asked Alma, her face full of concern.

'Yes, yes… It's just that…' Emily was going to offer an explanation but changed her mind. She didn't want to talk about Lucy; if she did, she might not be able to get herself to work. 'I was just a little surprised, that's all, and I didn't sleep well.'

'Of course you didn't, how could you?' Alma passed Emily her uniform. 'And I'm sorry to come barging in like this.'

'No, really, it's fine. I need to be prepared for the ward; you know what it's like on there.'

'I do, and I'm sure that a nosy American barging into your room first thing in the morning is the last thing you expected…

Anyway, like I was saying, we need to talk. The truth is, no one would blame you if you needed to take some time out, go back home to your folks... We all know how close you and Lucy were. If you need my help to ask Sister—'

'No, I couldn't do that... We're so short-staffed and Lucy would want me to keep going.'

'Sure, I understand that, but this flu is set to go on for some time, and it will probably get even worse before it starts to get better. I just think you should ask to take a break, get your strength back, you can always return to work later.'

'If it's getting worse then that's all the more reason for me to stay,' countered Emily, striving to keep her voice steady as she pushed her hair pins into place with extra vigour.

'I'm not going to argue with you, I know what a firecracker you can be,' Alma said with a reassuring smile. 'But I just need you to know that I've got your back. And if I think you're coming unstuck or this is all dragging you down too far, you know me, I will speak out.'

'Thank you.' A dark weariness started creeping back over her, threatening to pull her down. If she hadn't had sick patients waiting, she would probably have crawled back into bed and pulled the covers over herself. But she was determined not to go under. 'You're right, this is the toughest thing I've ever had to deal with – on top of everything else that's happening on the wards, it's enough to finish off the best of us. So, Alma, I think it's a good idea that you look out for me, and I'll keep an eye on you as well.'

'Deal' – Alma reached out a hand – 'let's shake on it.'

At the touch and warmth of Alma's skin, Emily couldn't rid herself of the memory of Lucy's cold hands – it was as if the sensation might haunt her for the rest of her life.

'Talk to me, Alma, tell me one of your stories,' she said, 'while I finish getting ready.'

'Well now, let me see… Did I tell you about the brand-new volunteer nurse I worked with at Ypres who passed out cold on her first day when she saw a basket full of amputated limbs?'

'No you didn't, and no wonder she fainted, that's awful for anyone!'

'We did feel a little sorry for her, but she'd flounced into camp like some ministering angel who knew everything about everything – not an ounce of training behind her. Lady Caroline, we called her. She was a snooty one; she'd joined the Red Cross thinking that all she'd have to do was mop the fevered brows of our brave soldiers. Anyway, she'd talked the talk the night before and made sure to tell us in great detail how well connected she was. So, yes, it was a shame that she fainted like that, but it also sort of served her right. At least after that, she listened up, she asked questions. To her credit, she toughened up and she spent a good six months with us until she was called home to a family emergency.'

'Sounds like she was a tough cookie after all. What happened with you, why did you come back?'

'Well, I think it had all started to drag me down a bit as well. This is probably a bit close to the bone for you – so tell me to stop if you don't want to hear – but I'd made a good friend out there, a British nurse called Violet, we clicked right from the first day. We were close to the front line so we got used to the rumble and roar and the screeching of shells… And then, one day she was working in one of the huts where we did the dressings and it was hit by a shell. She died instantly…'

Tears sprang to Emily's eyes.

'I'm so sorry, Emily, I shouldn't have told you that… what a ridiculous way to try and distract a nurse from her grief.'

'No, no, please keep going, keep talking…'

'Well, I managed to keep working but I never slept properly after that and the sound of the shelling… Anyway, one day another young soldier died in my arms and after that, I could tell that I definitely wasn't right. I was about to request a transfer back to England when a letter came from Aunt Foster telling me that she was sick and that she was probably at death's door... I'd had these letters before, usually they meant that she'd had too much port wine and I usually ignored them, but this time I took her up on it and I came back. She was completely fine of course and I started to feel better once I got away from the noise of war. Then, suddenly I was in at the deep end with Aunt Foster – afternoon teas, wondering which hat to wear, buying new clothes. All of the oh-so-trivial details helped me to get better, up to a point, but I knew that I needed to get back to nursing, so that's how I ended up here.'

'So you've had your struggles too... You always seem so bright and breezy, I would never have guessed that you'd had such a hard time.'

'Oh, no more than most. We're all boiling in the fires of hell when you think about it, aren't we?'

'Yes, I suppose we are... Tell me something else, another story from your training... I think it's helping...'

As they walked through the hospital, every time she heard a nurse running to catch up behind them, Emily felt her stomach tighten, expecting to hear the sound of Lucy's voice, breathless and excited.

Grace met them as they came through onto the ward and took Emily in her arms. 'I'm coming back onto days tomorrow,' she said eventually, 'we've got a new night nurse starting on here and I'll be moving onto female medical.'

'That's good,' Emily replied, knowing that it was because of Lucy, but neither her nor Grace wanted to say the words. As they drew apart, Grace gave her a kiss on the cheek and offered a smile before she went on her way.

When Emily looked up, Sister Montgomery was gazing down the ward, her eyes full of concern, and she pulled down her mask. 'You all right, Nurse Burdon?' she called, her voice steady, professional.

'Yes, Sister,' Emily replied as she made her way up the ward with Alma. Sister nodded before pulling up her mask, gesturing for the nurses to gather for the report.

And in fact she had started to feel better, just being back on the ward, knowing that she would be putting all of her energy into caring for the patients, with no time to think about anything else. Just one thing bothered her, though, something that she hadn't really thought of much before. She had experienced now, first hand, that the masks and gowns they wore only offered so much protection. As the others donned their gowns, ready to start work, she felt a prickle of fear. She would never shy away from fighting to save the lives of her patients, but having seen Lucy die so quickly, she would make sure to wash her hands more often, and say a prayer every hour if need be, that no more of the nurses died.

The ward was busy, as always. Once the day started, they were running from bed to bed – sponging patients down, sitting them up, wrestling them back into bed and recording pulse and temperature. Later on, as Emily stood packing pillows behind a wheezing patient whose fever had just begun to break, Sister Montgomery came to the other side of the bed to assist. 'That's the spirit,' she said and Emily could see that her eyes were smiling above her mask. 'You have remarkable courage, Nurse Burdon.'

She was only doing what any of the nurses worth their salt would have done – getting back to work as soon as possible. She started to shake her head in reply, but then it was as if Lucy was there beside her, giving her a nudge in the ribs, saying, *Don't be daft, of course you're doing well*. It felt strange to hear Lucy's voice so clearly, to feel her present. It made her smile. 'Thank you, Sister,' she said, not completely sure if it was her own voice that was answering or not.

She was still smiling as she moved to her next patient. For once Sid Wilkins was sitting up in bed, looking around and paying attention. He'd been knocked out by the flu for days and had been very disorientated and hallucinating, like many of the patients. But when he'd come round, he was strangely lucid and seemed to have lost most of the shell shock that he'd been suffering from. It was just what Emily needed, seeing him alert and able to answer questions; it felt like they'd had a real breakthrough with him.

On her way to lunch, she called by the nurses' pigeonholes, just in case there was a letter from Lewis – she hadn't heard from him since before the armistice. Her breath caught when she saw the familiar envelope. She knew there might be news of his return.

Ripping it open as she stood, she struggled to decipher the writing at first and then her hand flew up to her mouth. He was in a hospital at Dunkirk and he had the flu. She read it through again, realising that at least he was well enough to write. He said that he was recovering, but she knew all too well how quickly things could change. He was asking her to see if there was a bed at the St Marylebone, so he could come to her in London. He'd be shipping out in a few days so he needed her to send an urgent telegram to the military hospital to secure his place.

Her head was spinning with the news. All she could think of was that she needed to find James, that he would be able to help. She hadn't seen him on the ward so far and this couldn't be left to chance. As if to drive home the urgency of Lewis's request, some stretcher bearers ran past her in the corridor with a soldier coughing his guts up. Alma was right, they'd had even more admissions today and now Emily could see why Sister had been talking about putting some mattresses on the floor to create more space. She hoped that there would be a bed for Lewis.

All thought of any lunch now gone from her head, she went straight out to the back of the hospital to the abandoned tennis court to see if James was there. He wasn't, and the place seemed even more desolate, surrounded by the skeletons of the almost leafless trees. She made herself stand for a few moments and breathe in the cold air, hoping it would clear her head.

As she headed back along the corridor, wondering if she should drop by the doctors' mess to see if he was in there, she saw him approaching in the opposite direction.

He smiled instantly. 'How are you doing? Are you all right to be back on the ward so soon?'

'Yes,' she said, 'I wouldn't have been able to even try to stay away, knowing how busy we are. Have you seen it in there today?'

He was shaking his head. 'I know, we might have to put a stop on admissions at this rate.'

'In that case, I'm not sure if I should be asking this question or not but I'm going to anyway…'

'What is it?'

Emily felt her throat tighten, the last thing she wanted to do was ask James, of all people, for a favour. She never liked the idea of using your own position to get special treatment but she didn't see what else she could do. Lewis had asked specifically and it would cause her no end of anxiety if he was shipped off somewhere else.

She took a deep breath and came straight out with it, feeling two spots of colour start to burn on her cheeks as she spoke. 'Is there any chance that you could find a bed for my fiancé? He's on his way back from the front line and he's ended up in hospital with the flu.'

She saw him start in surprise and he took a step back from her. He stood for a moment, his mouth hanging open.

'I didn't know you had a fiancé,' he stammered, at last. 'I mean, yes, well, of course, given your circumstances, of course we could try and find a bed for him…'

She tried to look him in the eye, but he dropped his gaze and continued to stare at the floor. She could feel her cheeks still burning at the awkwardness between them. She so wished that she hadn't had to ask him like this. She would rather have come out and told Sister Montgomery about Lewis.

With no choice but to stand her ground, she continued, 'I've, erm, I received a letter from him today… and he needs a telegram to be sent to the military hospital at Dunkirk.'

He looked up at her. 'Yes, of course,' he said, his voice business-like now. 'Well, as you know, we are very busy, so I can't promise that there will definitely be a bed, but I will send the telegram asking them to transfer him here – if there is no capacity then we will, of course, have to move him on to another London hospital… What's his – your fiancé – what's his name?'

'He is Sergeant Lewis Dupree,' she said, feeling traitorous even saying his name. 'That's Dupree spelt d-u-p-r-double e.'

'Right, yes, thank you Nurse Burdon, I'll remember that, and I will keep you informed.'

'One other thing,' she said, feeling her breath catch as the reality of the consequences of her disclosure dawned. 'I don't want anyone else to know about this, please can you keep it secret?'

He started to reach out a hand to her but thought better of it. 'Yes, yes, of course I can, as far as anyone else is concerned, he will be just another one of our men returning from the front.'

'Thank you…' Emily said, straightening up, feeling a little lighter now that she'd made her request.

As he strode away from her, she shook her head wearily. If only Lucy was there to console her. She could always put things into perspective.

Immediately, she felt the now familiar sliver of pain, she almost cried out in despair as a fresh wave of grief washed over her.

Emily was alive with anticipation and watched out for James to come back onto the ward with a reply, but there was no sign of him for the rest of the day. Coming off duty with Alma, she made her excuses – rather than heading back to the nurses' home with the rest, she would go up to the lying-in ward to check on baby Jacob. And maybe James would be up there too…

When she pushed open the door, the room was empty apart from the little baby lying inside his glass box. She walked over, transfixed, and sat down on the chair beside the incubator. He was sleeping and she had every opportunity to study him through the glass. One tiny, perfect hand was stretched out, escaping from the blanket, and he had a tuft of wispy pale brown hair sticking up from his head. His breathing seemed steady and his colour was now much better. When he snuffled a little and blinked open his eyes for a second, she could have sworn that he was looking straight at her. 'You little beauty…' She placed the palm of her hand against the glass. Just the sight of him made her feel calm.

The door clicked open behind her and Nurse Berry entered closely followed by a middle-aged woman with dishevelled grey hair and tear-filled eyes. 'Ah, Nurse Burdon,' she said, her voice bright and her eyes creasing up at the corners with pleasure. Emily stood up from the chair and took a few paces towards her as the middle-aged woman walked slowly over to the incubator. 'This is Mrs Harvey, the baby's grandmother.'

'He's just like his father was when he was a baby,' the woman said, her voice quavering. 'It's like seeing my Edwin all over again.'

Nurse Berry leaned in to speak quietly to Emily. 'Edwin was her eldest son, he was killed six months ago, and her youngest died on the Somme.'

It was dizzying to contemplate the scale of this woman's loss.

'I can take him out of there, Mrs Harvey, if you want to hold him,' Nurse Berry offered.

The woman pressed a hand to her chest and she looked like she might collapse. Emily steadied her, steering her to the chair.

'There you go…' Nurse Berry turned with the baby in her arms. Mrs Harvey reached out to take him and in moments she was rocking him gently. She glanced up, a single tear escaping down her cheek. 'He is so like his Daddy.'

'This nurse was with your daughter-in-law when she died,' said Nurse Berry.

'Were you?' The woman's eyes were wide, expectant.

'Yes, I was… We did all that we could to save her, but it was just too late.'

'Poor Rose, she walked out of the house that day to go and see a friend, another young mother who'd lost her husband at the front, and she never came back. I went to the police stations and all of the hospitals. It's taken me days to track her down… only to find that she's dead and gone.'

'I'm so sorry for your loss…'

The woman nodded and then she looked back down to the baby. 'She's been like a daughter to me, Rose, with both my boys gone, and she had no family of her own. She would have been a wonderful mother… and so proud of this little one.' Her voice caught on a sob, 'He is so perfect.'

'We've called him Jacob,' Nurse Berry said kindly, 'but of course you can choose your own name for him.'

'No, Jacob is a good strong name,' she said, looking up, 'and it was given to him by those who saved his life. He will be Jacob.'

Emily couldn't wait to tell James about the turn of events, that Jacob had been found by his family. As she left the lying-in ward, she felt compelled to go to him straightaway… but maybe not… not yet. Clattering along the corridor, she ran to the pigeonholes again to see if there was any further communication from Lewis. There was an envelope for her, but it hadn't been posted. When she took it in her hand, she could feel the quality of the paper and her name had been written with a definite flourish. It all looked so nice that she didn't want to rip it open in her usual way; instead she carefully peeled it back.

Dear Nurse Burdon,

I have had a reply via telegram from the Dunkirk hospital and they have assured me that Sergeant Dupree will be on the next convoy across the channel. They expect him to arrive here, at the St Marylebone Infirmary, by tomorrow evening at the latest. If there is a vacant bed on the military ward I will arrange admission for him there directly.

Yours sincerely,
Dr James Cantor

Its formality took her by surprise, despite their awkward exchange in the corridor she hadn't been prepared for this. She'd thought that they were friends, but the tone of this letter seemed to undermine all of that. She swallowed hard – in the scale of things, this had to be something that wasn't going to make much difference, but she had so enjoyed the conversations that they'd had. She folded the letter, careless of the expensive paper now, and shoved it in her pocket.

She felt even more abandoned as she walked towards the nurses' home, struck afresh by the heavy truth that she wouldn't be able to share her troubles with Lucy. She needed to try and take her mind somewhere else, so as she walked she counted the steps in her head, like she used to as a child. It helped but she could still hear the sound of Lucy running up behind her, calling her name.

When Emily arrived at the nurses' home, Sister Kelly stepped out of her room. 'How are you, Nurse Burdon?' That was all that it took for the tears to come and she needed to be led into Sister's office so that she could sit down. A fire flickered in the hearth and as she sat gratefully in an armchair, Sister busied herself with the kettle that was warming on the hot plate and the cup of sweet tea that she readily provided without being asked.

There was nothing that Emily could say, she just sat with tears streaming down her face.

'I think you have done incredibly well to have worked today, Nurse Burdon. I can't imagine how hard it has been for you. And just so you know, I've had word back from Lucy's family this afternoon, and they want to have her home, for a burial at the village church. It hasn't been easy, given the sheer volume of deaths in the city at present, but I have managed to secure transfer of her body to Yorkshire. She will be leaving first thing.'

'I'm glad that she's going home,' Emily croaked.

Sister slipped into the opposite chair. 'So am I… My dear, normally, as you know, we nurses would have our own service of memorial, but due to the current constraints, that won't be possible. All I can suggest is that you come here, to me, and we say some prayers together or you go up to the Infirmary chapel for some quiet reflection.'

Emily wiped her eyes with the flat of her hand. Lucy would laugh her head off if she found out that Emily had been hunched up with Sister Kelly saying prayers. She almost caught the sound of her laughing now and it made her smile inside.

She drank the rest of her tea quickly, so as not to exhibit what might be construed as inappropriate behaviour. As soon as the tea was drunk, she was back in control. She placed the cup in the saucer with a decided chink. 'I'll go to the chapel,' she said, getting up from the chair. 'That's what Lucy would have wanted.'

CHAPTER 11

There were a number of empty beds on the ward the next day – one patient discharged and some more soldiers who had died from the flu. Two were filled instantly, as soon as the beds had been disinfected and made up with fresh sheets. The other stood tantalisingly empty and Emily was praying that it would still be there when Lewis arrived. She'd had no further communication from James and he hadn't been on the ward but he'd said that Lewis would be with them by evening at the very latest, so maybe there would be a chance of them securing this bed.

Emily threw herself into her work to keep distracted. The bustle of the ward, the nurses running back and forth, and Sister shouting over and over reminders to – *Pull up your mask... Don't lean over the bed if a patient is coughing* – punctuated every hour.

Then, a new admission came through the door. Her heart sank when she saw that the stretcher held a thin, hollow-cheeked man. She felt for him, being in such a poor state, but it was hard to reconcile that this man would take the last empty bed. Emily pushed down her disappointment and ran to help the stretcher bearers transfer him. Only when she got up close did she recognise the pale brown hair. She gasped, glad that she was wearing a mask to cover her shock. *Lewis.*

As they transferred him onto the bed, he started coughing and he opened his eyes, looking straight at her, and yet his eyes were blank, showing no sign of recognising her. She wrenched down her mask and she was sure that she saw a light of recognition, but then his body was convulsed by a coughing attack. Emily was fighting with his pillows, desperate to get him sat up high in the bed.

Sister Montgomery appeared at the other side of the bed. 'Pull your mask up, Nurse Burdon,' she instructed, before helping her settle the new admission.

'This is Sergeant Lewis Dupree,' one of the ambulance crew was saying, his voice steady, matter-of-fact. 'A confirmed case of flu with subsequent pneumonia, he wasn't expected to survive the crossing but as you can see, he's still here.'

Emily couldn't let Sister see how the words had hit her like a punch. She busied herself with the sheet and kept her gaze down so that Sister wouldn't see the tears.

'He must be tough this one, Nurse Burdon, a real fighter,' Sister said as she moved away quickly to the bed of the man opposite who was urgently calling for a nurse.

Emily picked up Lewis's wrist and felt for his pulse. It was racing like the fragile heart of a tiny bird. She made a recording and then still gripping her pocket watch, she listened carefully to each breath, counting his wheezy respirations. She felt a dull ache behind her eyes as she fully realised just how compromised his breathing was. The heat of the fever radiated from his body and his lips were cracked and dry – he was very dehydrated and she needed to get some water inside of him, otherwise he would definitely sink even lower.

She shook his shoulder. 'Come on Lewis, wake up, I need you to drink.' He groaned and then drifted back to whatever place he'd been in. 'Lewis,' she insisted, putting her arm beneath his head and shoulders and propping him up a little. 'Lewis, you *have* to drink or you won't get better.' He groaned again, moving his head from side to side. She had the cup to his lips but he wouldn't drink and the water was spilling down his chin. She had no choice but to be firm.

She tipped the cup. 'Swallow…'

His face creased in agitation but he had no choice. She repeated the action and he took some more. 'That's good, you're doing well.' He was trying to reach up now to grab the cup and she knew that she needed to give him a break. She laid his head gently back onto the pillow and as she smoothed back the lock of hair that lay damp on his forehead, he opened his eyes and stared straight at her.

'Lewis,' she said, feeling her heart jump a beat when she saw a flash of the man whom she knew.

He furrowed his brow trying to focus, his pupils dilated, and he started to mutter something – a name she couldn't make out but he definitely wasn't saying Emily.

'You're safe now,' she said. 'They've brought you to the Marylebone and you're with me, Emily. I'll look after you…'

His eyes were closed now and his face looked more relaxed – the sound of her voice, muffled as it was by her mask, had broken through. But she had no time to stand there thinking about whether he recognised her or not. There was work to do.

She fetched a number of flannels and a bowl of tepid water, dipping the inside of her wrist onto the surface to check the temperature and adding just a splash of hot to take the chill off – too cold water was a shock to the system and could make a patient shiver. Selecting the softest flannel, she soaked it and then squeezed out the excess water, before gently wiping around the contours of his face. She used a separate cloth for his poor dry lips, and then dipped the flannel again and wrung it out, straightening and folding it to place carefully on his forehead. When she stripped off his pyjama jacket, first at one side and then the other, she was shocked by just how thin he was. His ribs were protruding and his skin was dry, stretched like parchment. She recognised the pattern of hair on his chest, but this could have been the body of any other soldier, so unfamiliar it otherwise now seemed. She gritted her teeth as she wiped over his torso with the damp flannel, leaving the water to evaporate and help cool his body. Wringing out two more cloths, she placed one in each armpit. She could have cried when she saw the softening of muscle on his bicep; Lewis had always been proud of his strong arms and he'd grown up training to be a blacksmith. When she pulled the sheet up from the bottom of the bed, his legs were the same, so thin they looked like they could break. Forcing herself to be business-like, she sponged his legs and his feet, calloused from so many years of marching in ill-fitting army boots.

By the time she had given him more drinks of water, he was ready for a change of position to stimulate his breathing. She saw Alma passing by and called her over to assist. 'He looks poorly, our new patient,' said Alma, her face knotted with concern, 'he might not make it.'

Emily nodded, unable to speak as she felt the shock of it spoken out loud.

'Just keep doing what you're doing, there's nothing more that we can offer,' Alma rallied, turning on her heel to race across the ward as one of the other new admissions started to struggle out of bed, coughing convulsively.

When Emily took Lewis's temperature again it was satisfying to note that it had come down a couple of notches – the tepid sponging seemed to be working. As she took up the bowl to go for more water, the sound of a decisive footstep coming up the ward made her look up. It was James in his white coat, a stethoscope in his hand, heading in her direction. She put the bowl back down and glanced at Lewis's face, he appeared to still be in a semi-conscious state.

James was at the bottom of the bed, his eyes above the mask neutral, but he raised his eyebrows before he spoke. 'So, Nurse Burdon, our new patient has arrived.'

'Yes, Dr Cantor,' she said, meeting his gaze firmly, not wanting him to catch any glimmer of her being unsettled. What did she care now anyway? 'I've been tepid-sponging and his fever has started to come down,' she offered as James strode to the opposite side of the bed.

There was some warmth in his eyes when he looked at her again, his face intent as he slipped the stethoscope into his ears and proceeded to move it across Lewis's chest. His brow furrowed as he concentrated, glancing up with a look of regret after he'd checked and double-checked one particular area. He straightened up and his voice was solemn when he spoke. 'He does have some consolidation throughout the right lung – it might be an extension of the pneumonia that they identified in France. It's not looking—'

'Yes, I understand the significance,' she cut him off before he could tell her just how desperately ill Lewis was. She couldn't bear to hear it spoken out loud as he lay there on the bed between them, completely helpless.

James nodded. 'It might be worth trying a linseed poultice over his chest to try and loosen the phlegm…' he said, furrowing his brow.

She suddenly felt irritated with him – of course she would try that, had he not seen what they'd been doing on the ward all these weeks? She paused before she spoke, knowing that her whole body was on a razor-sharp edge of anxiety, and she made sure that her voice was steady before she replied. 'Yes, of course, I will try that. And thank you, Dr Cantor… for arranging the transfer… It means a great deal to me to have him here at the hospital. I do appreciate it.'

He gave a single nod of his head and when he looked at her again, his eyes above the mask were full of sympathy – clearly, he was expecting the worst outcome for Lewis. With his gloomy prognostications, she simply wanted him gone from the bedside.

Once she had the linseed poultice carefully applied, she had no choice but to move on straight away to other patients, helping out where she could. Each time she passed his bed, she glanced to check him – as she did with all the other patients. It felt strange, now that she'd been busy away from his bedside, because that's how he seemed – just another patient. Once she was back there, close up, the reality would hit her again, and the burden of that reality, sitting on her shoulders, made her feel even more exhausted.

Sister Montgomery always made sure that all of the nurses took regular breaks away from the ward if time allowed, even if it was just for five minutes in the day room or anywhere else away from the constant coughing, commotion and calling out of the patients. Emily was torn when it was time for her break from the ward. She wanted to sit by Lewis, but she wouldn't be able to do that without telling everyone why he was special. She wasn't ready to do that yet – it would take too much out of her and she certainly didn't want Sister starting to think differently about her, as someone who was just biding her time until she could go off and get married. She'd sworn James to secrecy and she trusted him not to tell anyone, even Alma.

There was only one place that she wanted to go for her break and it felt strange to be going up there voluntarily now. As she climbed the steps to the Infirmary chapel, she realised that she hadn't been back since that day when she'd broken another thermometer and been reprimanded by Sister. It felt as if it had happened in a different lifetime. When she opened the door, she admired the familiar patterned blue, cream and orange tiles on the walls and the stone arched windows, but when she pulled down her mask, the air in the room felt different. It was closed up, stale. Like no one had been in here for days – there was no time for proper services, not any more. Feeling stifled, Emily went straight to open a window so that she could get some air moving. She stood breathing in the cool breeze, listening to the sound of voices and passing traffic from the darkening street below. She couldn't remember the last time she'd walked out there and it made her feel confined, like a prisoner, hearing the life that was still going on outside the walls of the hospital.

Looking to the spot on the hard floor where she'd often knelt and vented her fury when she'd been sent here for some misdemeanour, she was momentarily tempted to get down on her knees again just to feel the pain, in the hope that it would make her feel more alive, more able to manage the work. Who would have thought, only weeks ago, that something even more terrible than the war was coming down the line. *We'll get through it, one day it will all be over*, that's what people kept saying, but right now, it was so hard to see the light at the end of the tunnel.

She slipped into a shiny wooden pew, trying her best to relax, but the hard pews weren't meant for comfort and she could only sit ramrod straight. *No wonder Sister always sent me up here*, she thought, starting to feel a little relief just thinking back to those innocent days before the flu came, when she didn't have much else to worry about apart from broken thermometers and Sister's bad temper.

She rested her hands on her waist for a few moments, feeling some stillness start to settle, becoming more grounded, and then she slid them down over her belly – she'd always been slim but now her hip bones were jutting out and her uniform was loose around her waist. *You need to get some food inside you*, she said to herself. She couldn't remember when she'd last eaten something proper – it must have been before Lucy died.

Lucy. Emily always tried to picture her smiling, to see the light in her friend's eyes; but all she ever had was the image of her gasping for breath.

'I'm so sorry,' she said out loud, 'I'm so sorry that I couldn't save you.' She closed her eyes, squeezing them tight. When she opened them and looked up, the Madonna, wrapped in her pale blue gown, was looking down with her beatific smile, as if she knew and understood all of the sorrows in the world. Emily met the gentle certainty of her gaze. 'I know what you're going to say,' she murmured, 'and many others have said the same. *It wasn't your fault, you did all that you could.*'

Still gazing at the Madonna, transfixed by her face, Emily felt a sense of calm settling over her and a dawning realisation that it really wasn't her fault. She couldn't have done any more for her friend. She glanced to the window, taking in another breath of fresh air as the sound of the voices in the street below drifted over her. The world was still turning, despite the pandemic; they all just had to keep going and then things would start to fall back into place. That was how life was.

In the next breath she thought of Lewis. Getting him here so that she could look after him, it was as if they'd had a helping hand. She glanced back to the Madonna and offered her a smile. As a child she'd attended the village church every Sunday, she would say the words, sing the hymns. And now, well, she was just too exhausted to wonder if there really was a God. But she knew one thing for sure, there was no mistaking the sense of calm that she felt, here in the chapel. She breathed it in and held onto it, just for a moment longer, resting back on the pew as her mind stayed with Lewis. With it came a flash of the young man she'd grown up with, who'd proposed to her one hot, summer's day just before the war. Picking a buttercup to hold beneath her chin, so that he could see the golden reflection on her skin, he'd asked, 'Will you marry me?' She could see his smile and his clear blue eyes, the warmth and the love that he had back then. 'Yes,' she'd said without even thinking as he took her in his arms. And now, here he was in a hospital bed, waiting for her to tend him. How strange life could be.

Her legs felt weak as she descended the stairs from the chapel and as soon as she reached the bottom, she saw James heading along the corridor in her direction. He was walking quickly, preoccupied, and for once he wasn't wearing a mask. She was struck again by how striking he was and remembered that first day they'd seen him and how Lucy had tried so hard to stop giggling. She thought it best to keep walking; he was so deep in thought that he probably wouldn't see her. But just as their paths crossed, he looked up and he cried out, 'Emily!'

'Yes?' she replied, stopping abruptly, feeling thrown out by the sudden change back to the James that she'd known before she'd told him about Lewis.

'Some good news,' he said. 'Our little baby, Jacob, he's gone home today with his grandmother – Mrs Harvey.'

Emily smiled instantly, feeling the joy much more acutely than she would have in normal times. 'That's such good news,' she said, wholeheartedly.

'Isn't it just?' There was a slight quaver in his voice, then she saw him take a hold of himself. 'I just thought I'd let you know, seeing as you had a share in his entry into this world and we, erm…' He was rubbing the back of his neck as if it were stiff. 'Anyway… I'm just going back to get my… stethoscope… then I'll be coming up to the ward.'

'Yes, of course… I need to get going anyway. Thank you for telling me about Jacob.'

She tried to decipher his expression – relief, possibly? Or was it something else? As she turned away, she heard the sound of his leather-soled shoes on the tiled floor as he walked briskly away towards the doctor's quarters. She didn't have time to think about what was so off key between her and Dr Cantor, she needed to get back to the ward, but whatever it was, she knew that in due course it would all probably come spilling out.

Straight back on the ward, she met Alma head on; her gown was hanging loose and, for once, her hair was slightly dishevelled. Emily could see that Alma was close to tears as she pulled down her mask and gasped, 'Sister's sending me off next, for a break. Another of my patients just died.'

'I'm so sorry,' said Emily, reaching out a hand to her.

'I'll be OK,' Alma tried to smile but her face looked rigid. 'I just need to take some time out.'

Emily gave her arm a squeeze before continuing on her way. She headed straight up the ward to check on Lewis, but for a moment she was thrown out, thinking she must have got the wrong bed. There was a woman kneeling beside this one, they weren't really supposed to admit visitors, but sometimes a distressed family member would break through and usually Sister was kind enough to let them spend a few minutes. Emily looked again as she got closer – yes it was Lewis's bed and the woman was weeping.

Poor thing, thought Emily, *she must have got the wrong patient.* She'd known this to happen before, especially with the flu cases; even in the space of a day the patients could look so changed. She went to the side of the bed, next to the weeping woman, noting her petite figure and head full of black, curly hair swept up in a loose knot. Emily spoke gently and then placed a hand on the woman's shoulder, 'I'm so sorry,' she said, 'but I think you must have the wrong patient.'

The woman looked up, wiping her eyes with the flat of her hand, and then she croaked, 'No... I don't think so... This is my fiancé. Sister directed me to this bed.'

Emily was shaking her head. 'No, I'm sorry... I can see that you are upset, and we are so busy it would be easy for Sister to make a mistake.'

The woman stood up now and pulled a handkerchief out of her pocket, wiping it around her face. When she looked at Emily again, her eyes were bright and a stray curl of black hair had fallen onto her forehead. She was beautiful. Emily waited, expecting her to nod her head and start looking around for the right bed but instead she leaned over Lewis as he lay there, oblivious to everything, and she reached out a gentle hand to smooth the hair back from his forehead. 'No mistake,' she said with certainty, glancing up with a smile, 'this is my fiancé, Lewis Dupree.'

Emily felt her chest heave as she gasped out loud and then her head was swimming. The world slid and tipped sideways and she could hear Sister's voice calling her name from what seemed like a very long way away.

CHAPTER 12

The light hurt as Emily blinked her eyes open. She couldn't think where she was, and then she saw Sister's frowning face looming over her and she thought she must be in some kind of trouble. She tried to get up; she was lying down on something hard, but it was all too much and now Sister was trying to speak to her but she couldn't catch what she was saying and her face was starting to go all blurry. She felt someone with firm hands take hold of her feet and lift them onto something soft. Her heart was thudding in her chest now and she was trying to take in a deep breath but her lungs felt stiff. *Don't say I've got it as well*, she thought fleetingly, before drifting off to some shadowy place where nothing made sense.

'Nurse Burdon,' said a man's voice, a nice voice. 'Nurse Burdon?' insisting now, and a firm hand was shaking her shoulder.

'What?' she groaned, trying to move her head and then attempting to open her eyes, but the light seemed so bright, like she was in an operating theatre. Her heart jumped a beat. What if she was dying, what if she was going to have an operation? She knew that she needed to get up and show them that she was all right and so she took a deep breath and then forced herself to open her eyes.

James was looking down at her, and he was smiling.

'You are so handsome…' she groaned, but her voice wasn't coming out properly.

'What was that she said?' snapped Sister's voice.

She heard James's laugh and then he said, 'Oh, I don't know, she's just coming round. Emily, Emily?' he said, patting her face.

'You mean, Nurse Burdon, don't you doctor?'

He laughed again and muttered something.

Emily sucked in more air and tried to sit up. This was all too much, having them looking down at her, talking over her. 'I'm fine,' she croaked at last, struggling up.

'Oh no you don't,' ordered James, using a hand to gently force her back down, 'You went into a dead faint – you looked awful. You're not ready to sit up just yet.'

'But what about the patients… I need to make sure…'

Then she remembered what she'd seen. She groaned, the memory of it flooding back, making her feel that she couldn't breathe. She wondered if that woman was still next to Lewis's bed, saying that she was his fiancée. Emily clung to the thought that the woman might still have been mistaken. But then, she'd said his name out loud…

'Emily?' She could hear the concern in James's voice but before she could say anything, her head was spinning again and her heart was thudding out of control.

'We need to get some sugar inside her,' she heard him call, before she slipped into oblivion once more.

When she woke, she was lying in bed and Alma was by her side. The light still hurt her eyes but she could at least see the shape of Alma's concerned face as she leant in with a feeding cup.

'Here, take some more of this,' Alma urged, pressing the cold, ceramic spout to her lips. Given the intent expression on her face, Emily didn't dare refuse, even though she felt sick. She swallowed down the sweet, sugary solution – it tasted ghastly. Alma was insistent that she take another mouthful and she did

as she was told but then she was coughing and she definitely felt
like she might vomit.

'Take some deep breaths. Now I'm going to help you onto
your side…'

Emily did as she was told and the nausea started to subside.
'Where am I?' she croaked.

'You're in your own bed. James carried you all the way from
the ward. He was going to take you to the sick bay but given
what happened there, I didn't want you waking up in the same
surroundings, so I directed him here.'

Emily slipped a hand down her body, she was in her nightie.
'Don't worry, I undressed you!' Alma laughed.

'Thank you,' said Emily, glad of Alma's intervention, but
feeling a warm flush on her neck. She told herself it was just
embarrassment because she didn't know if she'd left her nightie
or her underclothes scattered on the floor, but her heart had
already skipped a few beats just thinking about James, here, in
this intimate space.

'Right, madam,' said Alma, 'I've been given strict instructions
by Sister Montgomery and you have no choice in this.' Emily
tried to sit up, but she was still dizzy. 'You are to stay in bed and
meals will be sent to your room. Sister has been kicking herself,
telling me that she should have insisted that you stay away from
the ward after Lucy died. Anyway, too late for that now, she wants
you to *do as you are told*. She knows what you're like. And I agree,
you looked awful Emily, I was worried about you.'

'I'm sorry,' she said, reaching out a hand to her friend.

'Don't be sorry; just do as you are told.'

Emily smiled and propped herself up on one elbow. 'But what
if I feel much, much better tomorrow?'

'You have no choice, Sister will only march you straight off
the ward if you turn up.'

It seemed that she was stuck; she would have to do it. But her main concern, of course, was Lewis. She toyed with the idea of telling Alma the whole story, but knew how Alma liked to revel in that kind of thing. And it would mean that she lost some degree of control over the situation. Instead, she made Alma promise to keep a special eye on the patient that she'd admitted today, Sergeant Lewis Dupree.

'Of course I will, I'll take over where you left off, as long as you keep your side of the bargain.'

Alma stayed by her side and made sure she had plenty of drinks until there was a tap at the door and a tray of food was delivered by a girl from the kitchen. Satisfied then that Emily could be left propped up in bed, tucking into some food, Alma finally conceded and left her alone. Emily thought that she'd only be able to nibble at the corner of the bread, but as soon as she started on the chicken broth, her stomach gave a rumble and she realised that she was starving. This was the first real food that she'd eaten for days.

Once the whole meal was gone, including a sticky lump of suet pudding, it was as though she could feel the life coming back. She sighed, rolling onto her side, leaving the tray exactly by the bed, as Alma had instructed. Sleep came to her then like a black curtain falling, sleep that she'd never had the like of since she was a small child.

A murmur of voices out in the corridor woke her. She blinked; it was morning and it sounded like the early shift were on the move. Emily groaned, thinking that she was going to be horrendously late. Then she remembered and rolled gratefully onto her other side and instantly fell back to sleep.

When she woke again a sliver of pale light was coming in through the gap in her curtains. She propped herself up on an elbow, testing to see if her head was steady. She felt fine, regretting her easy compliance with Sister's request now. Once she put her feet on the floor and stood up however, she had to admit that it had been the right decision – her legs felt weak and when she tried to walk, she was like a newborn foal, staggering across the room. A breakfast tray had been left on her dresser along with a note in Alma's bold hand propped by the side of the plate: *DO AS YOU ARE TOLD*. She smiled, feeling her stomach rumble, and she sat back down on the bed, enjoying the brief respite that she'd been forced to take.

After another lengthy sleep, she woke to a gentle knock on the door. She got out of bed, steady on her legs now, and opened up. One of the housekeeping staff was there with another tray of food. A shy young woman with a pink flush on her cheeks and a tentative smile. 'Sister Montgomery sent this and she told me to tell you not to even think about coming to the ward.'

Emily couldn't help but giggle, it was as if Sister could read her mind. 'Thank you,' she said taking the tray from the girl whose face was now almost scarlet.

She had no choice, she would have to comply, but she also had the urge to be up and dressed – she had to get out of this room. The food on the tray was polished off in double quick time and by the final crumb she had a plan – she would get her hat and coat on and go out into the city, she couldn't remember having been out since she'd walked with James to Bill Steadman's house… maybe she could call by and check how he was doing.

The blue wool coat that had fitted her properly last time she'd worn it now bagged around her waist and she felt slightly woozy, peeping out from under the brim of her matching felt hat. As she headed towards the archway that led out onto the street, she glanced up to the stained-glass windows of the chapel, wondering if she should have gone in there instead. But it was too late now, her innate stubbornness wouldn't let her change her course of action and there didn't seem any way to stop her heeled leather boots tapping a brisk staccato over the cobbles as she walked beneath the arch.

She wondered about trying to sneak onto the ward just to take a peek at Lewis, but that's when she realised the twist in her feelings towards him. *Why should I? Why the heck should I when he has been seeing that woman in secret? He must even have asked her to marry him…* She was sure now that what she'd witnessed was genuine, and she'd gone from trying to blot it out to going over and over it in minute detail. The woman's face was stamped in her mind, she couldn't budge it, and she bristled inside her wool coat knowing that once Lewis started to wake up, he would be facing some questions and maybe he would need to make a choice. *What will be, will be*, she told herself as she walked out into the street.

Less than twenty yards down Exmoor Street, she realised that she had probably made a mistake coming out so soon. For a start, many people were wearing masks and they were hurrying along, dodging out of the way of others as if fearing for their lives. She was a nurse, why hadn't she thought to wear a mask? It made her feel exposed, more vulnerable than she'd ever felt inside the walls of the hospital. She almost turned back, but then seeing a group of women without masks at the other side of the road, she kept going, knowing that her legs were starting to feel stronger already with the exercise.

Turning into the next street, the hairs prickled at the back of her neck – both sides were lined by a murmuring crowd and down the street she could see a funeral cortège approaching – a solemn procession flanked by men in dark suits and tall black hats. The whole street had fallen silent, all standing in quiet dignity. As she squashed in next to a well-dressed gentleman with grey hair, she caught a strong waft of eucalyptus. He had no mask but was using a handkerchief scrunched to his nose. He glanced at her in alarm, but she could feel the press of people behind her and she had no choice but to stay right where she was.

The cobbles were strewn with straw to muffle the sound of the horses' hooves; all proper respect was being paid. Emily heard a child's whimper nearby and she pressed a hand to her chest. As the cortège came nearer she could see that there were two vehicles. First, a gun carriage carrying a coffin draped with a union flag, an army cap resting on top. As one, all of the men removed their caps and a collective held breath was palpable as silently they stood with their heads bowed.

The next vehicle approached – a large glass hearse pulled by two dark bay horses with plumes made from black ostrich feathers. The only sound apart from the rumbling of the carriage was the jingle of the harness. One woman sobbed and it caught, spreading down each side of the street. There were many sobbing now, the sombre-faced men still clutching their caps, and women dabbing at their eyes with white handkerchiefs. Emily wanted to look away but her eyes were drawn to the glass hearse and the coffin. She held back a gasp when she saw a much smaller coffin tucked alongside. Tears were coursing down her cheeks now and she pulled her own handkerchief out of her pocket.

As the group of mourners, led by two women in black veils and a man wearing a black armband, trudged inevitably by, the cortège started to turn at the bottom of the street, and the onlookers began a murmur of conversation. Two women were saying quietly that it was a family – he'd been an army officer and he'd come home from the front to find his wife and five-year-old daughter dead in their beds from the flu. In two days he'd passed away from it as well. Emily knew that she needed to move, to keep walking, but she was still trapped by the crowd. Thankfully, the grey-haired man next to her replaced his hat, and then he started to gently shoulder his way out. At last she could escape.

Emily's heart was aching as she picked up her pace, desperate to get away. Turning into the next street she almost collided head on with two men wearing blunt pointed masks that made them look like strange birds. They were sloshing carbolic solution around on the pavement and scrubbing at it with brushes, clearly attempting to disinfect. The tangy smell met her nostrils as she dodged around them, desperate to be on her way.

Further along she saw some children's toys – a wooden hoop and a hobby horse – discarded in the street. She caught the sound of a child shouting but it seemed distant, almost ghostly. And then she heard a wailing cry through the open door of a terraced house and she saw two bearers, a man and a woman, carrying out a shrouded stretcher. A dark-haired girl of about seven with a bow in her hair that matched her blue pinafore bolted out of the house, chased by an older woman. The child was screaming and shouting, 'I want my mummy, I want my mummy!' The older woman was in tears, holding onto her. 'Your mummy has gone,' The girl was angry and spitting, struggling to break free. 'Where has she gone? I want my mummy!'

Emily was about to offer assistance but the child was clinging to the woman now, watching as the men loaded the stretcher onto the flat back of a cart, pushing it into place alongside three others.

Emily walked by quickly, not even knowing if she was going in the right direction for Bill's house. She had to stop, her stomach was heaving and she needed to take deep breaths to hold back the nausea. She couldn't go any further. Turning around so that she wouldn't see the cart, she took some more deep breaths, and quickly started to retrace her steps.

A feeling of relief flooded her as soon as she saw the yellow brick towers of the hospital buildings. She waited impatiently for an open-topped omnibus crammed full of people wearing masks to pass by, so that she could cross the road. As a man struggled to the door of the bus, a handkerchief over his mouth, he gave one loud, explosive cough. Emily shuddered, dodging across the street, through the horse-drawn vehicles, motor cars and a taxi cab, all held at bay by a tall policeman in a silver-buttoned uniform. He nodded as she flitted past, his expression indecipherable behind his mask.

Emily walked briskly the rest of the way, her eyes firmly fixed on her destination. But then she halted, frozen to the spot – a small woman with black, curly hair was also bustling towards the hospital entrance. There was no mistaking who it was, it was the woman who had been by Lewis's bed. But what Emily hadn't been prepared for was the child who was trotting along beside her, smiling up to the woman as she held her hand. The little girl also had a head of dark curly hair, just like her mother, but as they moved towards her, Emily could see the shape of the girl's face and her big blue eyes. There was no mistaking it; the girl was the spitting image of Lewis.

The woman gave her a quizzical glance as she got closer, but clearly, she didn't recognise her out of uniform. All Emily could do was stand frozen and watch them walk in through the archway. As soon as they were gone, a hollow space inside of her filled with so much rage she could have exploded. Her instinct was to go straight to the ward, there and then, to have it out with the woman. But she knew already that it wouldn't serve any purpose, the woman and the little girl were as unaware of her existence as she had been of theirs yesterday. She would have to bide her time, wait for Lewis to come round. Knowing that he was still gravely ill didn't make her any less angry with him and she knew that she would have to steel herself if she was going to be able to nurse him properly, just like any other patient. But as soon as he started to open his eyes and he was stronger, she wouldn't pull her punches.

CHAPTER 13

'All's well!' called Alma, bursting into Emily's room at the end of her shift. 'We managed without you – just about – and that new patient you asked me to keep an eye on – Lewis Dupree – he seems to be out of danger. He even rallied round enough to say few words.'

Emily felt her skin prickle. 'What did he say?'

'Oh, just his name and regiment, that kind of thing. He was more concerned about being infected with the flu, wanted to know if he was going to live… We told him yes – of course we did – and there is a strong chance now that that will be the case. He just has to live… That woman who visited him yesterday, she came again with a little girl of about three – a real cutie with black curly hair and big blue eyes. They didn't stay long and the woman looked a bit upset when she was leaving, probably overwhelmed by the whole thing, but the little girl, she was so sweet, she even gave me a wave and said "bye bye".'

Emily had a buzzing sound in her head, she felt off balance.

'Are you OK, you don't look so good.' Alma's voice seemed to echo. 'Let's get you sat down, that's it, you're as white as a sheet.'

'I'm alright,' she tried to say, knowing that she would have to be.

She heard Alma's voice again, this time clearer, 'Let's just pop your feet up on the bed.'

It was ridiculous that she was feeling like this and had to be treated like an invalid, she really did need to sort herself out –

she was damned if she was going to let Lewis come here to the Infirmary and render her next to useless, unable to work.

Emily forced herself to speak, made her voice clear. 'Really, I am okay.'

'Mmm, let me be the judge of that…' Alma picked up her wrist to feel for her radial pulse. 'It's very rapid…' There was a knot of anxiety between her eyes. 'I don't think you're going to be fit to go back to work tomorrow.'

'I will be fit!' Emily said forcefully, causing Alma to reel back.

'Whoa, tiger, let's just see how you are, hey?'

'I have to go to the ward tomorrow. We're short-staffed already; I can't leave you all stuck,' Emily pleaded.

'Of course you're thinking like that. I know how it is, I'd be exactly the same… But if I think you're not well enough in the morning, you need to listen – I don't want to be carrying you back here again.' Alma started to laugh then. 'You should have seen James's face, he looked so shocked and the way he carried you – like you were the most precious thing in the world. I bet he wouldn't carry me like that, he'd probably just sling me over his shoulder.'

Emily couldn't help giggling.

'There you go, you've got some colour back in your cheeks! I think if you get a good night's sleep you'll be just fine by the morning.'

Emily reached out a hand to her then, starting to feel something of the closeness that she'd had with Lucy. The words were on the tip of the tongue; she wanted to tell Alma everything about Lewis. But seeing her, pale with fatigue, she just couldn't – each of them needed all of their energy for the work, at least that's what she told herself. She knew deep down that Alma would have listened carefully, probably given her good advice, but it just felt too soon to have that level of intimacy with someone else – as if it would somehow be a betrayal of Lucy.

As soon as Alma had gone to her room there was a gentle tap at the door and before Emily could raise herself up from the bed, Grace stepped in. Seeing her concern, she made sure to stand up from the bed, just so that Grace would know that she was feeling better. 'Oh, it was just a faint, I'm fine!' Emily chirped, giving her a hug, 'I hadn't been eating properly after Lucy died, I was just light-headed.'

Grace narrowed her eyes. 'I'm just checking on you, that's all, and I can see that you've got your colour back, but that's not all there is to it, is it?'

How did Grace know? Emily was about to come out with some response but before she could utter a word, Grace continued, 'We've never had a time like this... On my ward two of the nurses have gone under with the strain of it all – working twelve-hour shifts, seeing death after death, and now another nurse has been infected. I know what you're like, Emily, you always soldier on, but I need you to know that you can talk to me at any time, this work that we are doing now is punishing. Are you really OK, really?'

'I am! I'm feeling much better.' Relieved that was all there was to it, Emily smiled in response. 'How are things on Female Medical?'

As Grace filled her in on the dreadful news of the young women who were dying on the ward, some of them leaving children behind, Emily knew that her own troubles were nothing in comparison. Grace was also concerned about her own family – her little sister, Molly, had fallen ill with a fever. She was going straight there to assess her condition.

Emily gave Grace another hug, trying to reassure her, but whatever she said couldn't possibly take away the fear that they all had, that one of their family members would get sick with the flu and die. And for Grace, who visited home regularly, how would she be able to live with the knowledge that she could well have carried the infection from the ward?

After Grace had gone, Emily stood in front of the mirror, staring at her reflection; she set her mouth in a firm line and spoke out loud to herself. 'I know that this is hard for you, this stuff with Lewis, but you will have to get on and deal with it. You need to be fit for work and you need to work hard.'

Pulling open the top drawer of her dresser, she rummaged through to find the framed picture of the young, smiling Lewis that she'd tucked away ages ago. Unrecognisable now, from the man who lay on the ward. She just needed to check that she hadn't been mistaken, that the man looking out at the camera was someone who she used to have a special bond with. Those eyes, that smile told her everything. But it didn't help, it just made her feel even more desolate. Angrily, she pushed the photograph to the bottom of the drawer, under some papers.

On top, she saw the most recent letter from her mother, received last week. She pulled it out of the envelope, needing to see the generous curves of her handwriting, hear the calm voice that the words conveyed. Once she started to read, she wished she'd chosen another letter. This one was telling her that although there'd been no cases of flu in the village, it was starting to invade the nearest town. At the time of first reading, Emily had told herself that a tiny rural village with only a small number of inhabitants, who never travelled anywhere apart from the livestock auction, was probably one of the safest places to be. But seeing the family funeral out in the street today had unsettled her – it had taken the disease out of the hospital and into the real world. Now, she had to accept that this fatal flu wasn't just confined to hospital cases, it was a threat to everyone, everywhere.

Emily made sure to muster a lively step as she made her way to the ward the next morning, Alma chatting non-stop behind her mask.

Grace had come to Emily's room earlier to tell her that the news from home was better than expected – Molly did have a fever and

she was poorly but now that the rash had come out they could
see that it was measles. *What a relief,* Grace had said, and then
they'd both exchanged a knowing glance – before the flu, they
would have been instantly worried, measles was still a killer of
small children. But Grace had said her mother was a very capable
nurse – the eldest of twelve, she'd helped nurse every single one
of her siblings through measles and diphtheria and chicken pox
and they'd only lost one of them, the very youngest girl who'd
always been the weakling of the family.

No wonder Grace is an incredible nurse, Emily thought as they
walked along, only half-listening to Alma's story. To have grown
up with a mother who had that kind of history… She remembered
then that her own mother had nursed Dad through his stroke.
And even back then, Emily had been the one who had taken to
it naturally, so no real surprise that she'd moved on to train as a
nurse whilst Alice and Lizzie had gravitated to the shop.

'—And after that first kiss, I never wanted to see him again!'
Alma was finishing her story, laughing. Emily was sorry that she'd
missed the content of that particular one but it was too late to
ask for a repeat performance.

A young soldier was standing outside the ward, it was Sid
Wilkins, as calm as you like, smoking a cigarette. She walked
straight up to him. 'It's nice to see you up and about, Sid.'

He grinned at her, still a little wheezy on his chest as he started
to speak. 'I'm off home to Manchester today,' he said. 'What do
you think about that?'

'That's such good news. Say hello to the North for me, will
you?' she said, feeling so happy, knowing that he was now being
discharged.

'I will that!' he called after her. 'And thanks for all you've done
for me, Nurse Burdon.'

*

Sister Montgomery raised a hand and gestured for Emily to join her at the top of the ward. Emily made sure to walk briskly, knowing that Sister was watching her every step. 'Nurse Burdon, it is good to have you back on the ward. Are you sure that you are well enough for this?'

'Yes, I'm sure,' Emily said, perhaps a little too forcefully.

She saw Sister's dark brows scrunch in a thoughtful frown for just a second and then the corners of her eyes turned up as she smiled. It took Emily by surprise and made her feel a little unsettled. Sister was gesturing now for all of the nurses to gather round but she reached out a hand to hold onto Emily's arm, making sure to keep her by her side.

Once they were all gathered, Emily noted Alma's smiling face. Whatever was going on, she was definitely a part of it.

'I just want us to take a few moments before report to give a special mention to our Nurse Burdon,' Emily heard her say. *Oh no*, she thought, *she's going to single me out for praise for coming back to work after fainting.* She didn't want any more attention to be paid to that particular event. But then Sister was reaching into her pocket and pulling something out. 'For all of us, the last couple of months have been a very difficult time… and I'm afraid that this is set to continue. I am proud of all of you nurses, but especially the probationers who stepped up early to take on more responsibility. The final phase of training is usually where a nurse knows her strengths and finds her speciality, there has been no space for this set to even think about it, but they have worked alongside their peers without complaint. So, without the usual conclusion to training, we ward sisters have taken it upon ourselves to present the hospital badges to the individuals who would have been qualifying at the end of the year.'

Knowing how excited Lucy had been about them passing without doing the test and how she wanted to have her badge, Emily had to fight to keep her composure.

'And so, nurses, I want you to witness this presentation to Nurse Burdon, one of the best, who has proved herself many times over during this current crisis.'

Emily could only think about Lucy and she made herself smile, knowing how proud she would have been of herself, of them both... Sister leaned in to pin the bronze badge, embossed with the image of the Madonna and child, firmly onto her apron. Once it was in place, Emily gently ran her fingers over it, feeling the lettering around the top edge that spelled out St Marylebone Infirmary.

'Well done, Nurse Burdon!' all of the nurses were congratulating her. As they received the report, Emily gently grasped the badge.

This is for you as well, Lucy, she said to herself.

It was a good job that Emily knew most of the patients off by heart because her mind was floating above somewhere all the time that Sister was speaking. She came to when Sister clapped her hands and shouted, 'Now nurses, let's get on. But first, please will someone get a window pole and open up the top windows, I know it's cold outside but we need to get the air moving through the ward.'

Emily was relieved to be assigned to work with Alma again, especially since they'd been allotted to Lewis's portion of the ward. Sister had reported that the night staff had been struggling with him – he'd had terrible nightmares, waking up and shouting for someone called Jim, and then sobbing and crying in his sleep. Emily had felt a stab of concern for him; she'd known for some time that he was traumatised by war but it sounded as though things were getting worse. She would have to speak to him today though; this situation with the mysterious dark-haired woman and her child was burning a hole inside of her.

Lewis had just been given fluids and had a change of position so all that she needed to do right now was heat up a linseed poultice and apply it. Making sure that it wasn't hot enough to burn, but a little warmer than normal, she walked to his bed. He looked fast asleep and she gently shook his arm. 'Lewis, it's me,' she said in his ear. He didn't show any sign of rousing so she lifted his pyjama jacket and slapped the poultice on, over the lower half of his chest. She was sure that he flinched but still his eyes were closed tight shut.

She pulled out her fob watch, attached to her pocket with a chain, and picked up his wrist to check his pulse. It was strong, but not bounding, and rather rapid. Still holding her watch, she observed the rise and fall of his chest, counting the number of breaths per minute. She couldn't be absolutely sure, but it did seem that his breathing was easier, maybe his chest was loosening. As if to answer her question he started to cough and she saw him bring something up and swallow.

'Lewis.' She gave his shoulder a shake. 'Lewis, I know you can hear me.'

Still he didn't open his eyes.

To stop herself from screaming at him, she took deep breaths, and eventually spoke. 'You made it Lewis, you're at the Marylebone, and you're getting better.'

'Emily,' he croaked, blinking in the light, and he was reaching for her hand. She knew that he was hedging his bets; he didn't even know whether or not she'd seen the woman visiting him. She could see how thin he was, lying there helpless on the bed, and he had tears at the corners of his eyes now. What else could she do but try to comfort him? She gave his hand a squeeze. 'I'll be back to see you again soon,' she said as gently as she could.

Seeing a patient across the ward about to fall out of bed, she bounded over to restrain him. 'Please can you do Sergeant Dupree's temperature for me?' she called out to Alma. 'I didn't quite manage to finish his observations.'

Alma nodded and went straight to the table in the middle of the ward where they kept the ward thermometers in antiseptic solution.

Emily felt like she'd had a reprieve as she grappled with the patient who'd now started to sing, 'Roses are shining in Picardy'. She joined in with the song so that she could get him settled back into bed; Sister was already on her way down the ward with some medicine for him. Glancing across to Lewis's bed she saw Alma leaning over him, clearly he was talking to her. It was unlikely that he was telling her that he was also engaged to Nurse Burdon, but it troubled her nonetheless, not knowing what was being said. She would have to confide in Alma, the sooner the better.

As soon as her patient was settled, she went along to the next, working with Alma to bed-bath a man who had been struggling with the flu for days, drifting in and out of consciousness. As they sponged him down, they spoke soothingly to him – telling him he was doing well. Given his wheezing breath and the violet discolouration of his face, Emily knew that his fate was already sealed and it would only be a question of time now for the poor man.

As they were finishing up, James appeared and walked straight over to Lewis's bed. Emily saw him speak and then he plugged his stethoscope into his ears and had a listen to Lewis's chest. As he walked back, he exchanged a glance with Emily.

'I just need to go and have a word with Dr Cantor about Sergeant Dupree,' she told Alma, walking purposefully across as he indicated for her to come with him to the bottom of the ward, where there was less chance that they would be overheard.

'I'm so sorry about what happened the other day,' he said solicitously. At first, she wasn't quite sure what he was going on about but then she realised that he must have seen the woman at the bedside and put two and two together. 'It must have been a terrible shock for you… and I believe that the woman came again yesterday with a child…'

She really didn't think that she wanted to be discussing this on the ward, it didn't feel right, but his face was earnest and, in the end, given that he had already patched together the story for himself, it felt something of a relief to have someone to confide in. 'Yes, it was awful,' she breathed. 'And, of course, given the state he's in, I haven't even had the chance to confront him yet.'

'Of course,' murmured James, 'but he does seem to be coming round now… Maybe you'll get a chance soon to find out what happened.'

She nodded. 'But please bear in mind that no one else knows about my situation apart from you.'

His eyes widened. 'I see… And I understand your difficulty. Do you want me to have a word with him?'

'No, of course not!' she blurted out, pulling her mask down now so that he could see just how bad an idea she thought that was.

'OK, but please let me know if you need any help.'

'I will. And don't say anything to Alma about this, not yet… I want to be the one to tell her.'

'Understood.' He reached up to touch her face, resting the palm of his hand gently against her cheek for a moment. She felt her heart surge but she was soon back in control when, glancing up the ward, she saw Sister fast approaching. Instantly he dropped his hand.

'Thank you for the update, Nurse Burdon,' he said loudly, too loudly not to arouse suspicion. 'Please keep me informed.'

As he took a step away, Emily winced when she saw Sister glance in her direction, her eyes narrowed. And as James took Sister's arm to lead her away, Sister glanced back again to where Emily stood pulling up her mask, still feeling the warmth of James's hand on her cheek.

*

Towards late afternoon Emily found herself back at Lewis's bed. Sister and one of the first-year probationers had turned him onto his other side and he was ready and waiting for the next poultice. She'd made it good and hot enough for him to feel the sting of it again and she stood weighing it in her hands, looking down at him as he slept like a baby. Of course she understood how very ill he'd been, of course she did. But seeing him lying there sleeping, oblivious, maddened her beyond belief.

'Lewis,' she said determinedly.

Instantly, he opened his eyes. She could see the slight recoil when he looked up at her.

Still holding the poultice, eye to eye with him, she knew that she was going to have to say something. 'I saw your visitor yesterday,' she said with cut-glass precision. 'That dark haired woman with a child, a little girl of about three?'

His eyes widened, and she knew him so well that she could see the mental calculations he was making.

'Oh, she was just a friend of mine from London—'

'Don't start coming out with some cock and bull story,' she hissed, struggling to keep her voice down. 'That child is the spitting image of you, there is no way that you can deny it.'

His eyes darted from side to side as he figured out what to say next. 'She means nothing to me, Emily, I swear. It was just a fling, an accident... I hardly know the woman.'

'Don't lie to me,' she growled, 'and don't treat me like an idiot... I could see the way that she was with you—'

With a glint of defiance in his eyes, as weak as he was, he changed tack. 'Well, what was I supposed to do? All you ever wanted was to go home to see your family and you know what it's like for me back there, with my Dad. I needed to find comfort somewhere.'

'Don't you *dare* blame me,' she spat, feeling like she could slap him.

She saw the shape of his mouth then and she knew that he was truly making himself believe that he was the unwitting victim in all of this.

'You are not getting away with this!' she said, forcing her voice to steady up, aware of a concerned glance from the patient in the next bed.

He closed his eyes then and pretended to be asleep. She went around to the other side of the bed and applied the poultice, wishing that it was still piping hot.

There was no sign of the woman and her child that day and so Emily avoided any further contact with Lewis, leaving his care to Sister and the new probationer. She knew that she was going to have to play this very carefully if she didn't want to risk disgracing herself in front of the whole ward.

Delayed with a new admission, another flu case, she was later off the ward than the rest of the day staff. As she walked alone through the corridor, she realised it was time to tell Alma about Lewis and the woman and the child. But she needed some fresh air first.

Walking out of the hospital it felt like a relief to be leaving behind the hard, reflective surfaces of the tiled corridor and the all-pervading smell of disinfectant. But she wasn't ready to go straight back to the nurses' home just yet. Moving quickly along the familiar path that led to the abandoned tennis courts, she saw her warm breath steaming in the cold air. It was dark, but some light from one of the buildings made things just about visible. The stars appeared frozen in the sky and the crescent moon hung there, reminding her of home.

Initially she didn't notice anything untoward, but then she heard a low murmur of voices and she saw a mist of steaming breath further along by the wire of the tennis court. She was about to turn away, not wanting to interrupt some private conversation, when she realised that the two people were very close by. The steam cleared for a couple of seconds and she saw blonde hair. Alma. She almost called out to her but then with a dull thud of realisation, she saw that she was entwined in the arms of a man, and that man was James.

Emily turned away immediately, walking quickly, feeling furious and humiliated, just like someone who'd been betrayed.

CHAPTER 14

'You OK, Ems? You look a bit peaky this morning,' Alma said, intervening between Emily and her mirror to check that every single strand of her own hair was exactly in place.

Emily had felt her skin prickle as soon as Alma had tapped on the door, and now, having her stand so close in her spotless uniform, she had to bite her tongue so as not to say something inappropriate. After all, what business was it of Emily's if her friend had had some secret liaison with Dr Cantor?

'I'm fine, just a bit tired,' she replied, keeping her voice steady. Alma frowned, creasing her perfect forehead, and she leant in closer, face to face, her green eyes sparkling with enquiry and genuine concern. 'Mmm,' she said, 'you do look a bit haggard, I hope you're going to be OK.'

'Of course I will.'

Alma was still frowning. She placed the back of her hand on Emily's forehead. 'You don't sound your usual self, but there's no fever. Have you got a headache, a cough?'

'No, honestly, I'm absolutely fine,' she repeated, feeling the twitch at the corner of her mouth that she always had when she was trying to stop herself saying something that she shouldn't. Her mother was aware of that twitch and she'd always told her to 'spit it out', whatever it was she needed to say.

Emily couldn't do that now, she knew that she couldn't. A whole dammed-up mess of rage would come flooding out – and she knew this wasn't all about Alma and James, most of it was down to the fact that Lewis was lying there in a hospital bed that she'd arranged for him, as he waited for a visit from another woman who had borne his child. She still hadn't got her head around it yet and there was no way on earth that she wanted to confide anything in Alma right now.

She made herself chat to Alma as they headed to the ward, with Grace walking quietly at her other side. Mercifully, Emily was put to work at the opposite end of the ward today and given the responsibility of supervising the probationer. She didn't have to attend to Lewis, which was good because the way she was feeling she just might strangle him. And she was away from Alma – who, infuriatingly, kept waving and smiling from the other end of the ward. Emily waved back – what else could she do? – but if Alma approached anywhere nearby, she made sure to be engrossed in something with her probationer. Nurse Hooper was a sweet girl with an open smile and a willingness to learn, but she was also on the clumsy side, so she did need close attention. She reminded Emily of herself, on her first ward, with Lucy…

'Nurse Burdon, are you all right?'

'Yes, Sister!' she shouted back, busying herself instantly. 'Come on Nurse Hooper, I want you to make a linseed poultice for our patient in bed three…'

And so the day went by. Dr Cantor briefly appeared on the ward and looked in her direction, but she pretended not to see him. She also knew that she would have to confront Lewis again; she kept looking at him, sat there, but each time her stomach clenched with anger. She needed to be much calmer if she was going to be able to speak to him properly.

Emily thought the moment might come at visiting, but then the woman appeared again with the child by her side. As she came down the ward, she was walking slowly with her head down, almost dragging herself along.

Emily couldn't hide her distraction – even Nurse Hooper was asking Emily if she was all right. Emily told herself not to look, but her eyes were drawn to Lewis's bed. He kept glancing up and down the ward; he was definitely on his guard and he was barely taking any notice of the woman who was now standing patiently by his bedside. Emily saw the sweet little girl keep glancing up to her mother.

Right then, even amidst the clamour of the ward and the coughing of the patients, Emily heard a murmur of concern and then the child was screaming. Emily ran down the ward towards Lewis's bed to find the woman on the floor, gasping for breath, with the little girl clinging to her, sobbing.

Instantly Emily assessed the situation. She felt at the woman's forehead – she had a fever and she was starting to cough, white froth coming out of her mouth. There was no mistaking the signs. Emily heard Lewis saying something, asking if the woman was all right. 'I don't know,' she shouted up at him.

Alma rushed to help and they exchanged a glance; they both knew the score, especially for a patient who collapsed so suddenly with severe symptoms. Alma soothed the girl, while she clung to her mother, howling. 'It's all right, sweetie, it's all right, we're going to look after your mommy.'

'The side room is empty!' called Sister, striding rapidly down the ward. 'Let's take her in there for now. I'll get a porter with a stretcher.'

Emily thought it best to leave the woman where she lay for the time being and Alma handed Emily some swabs so that she could clear her mouth. Once her airway was unobstructed, her breathing was a little easier, but then she sneezed violently and a spray of blood came from her nose. Emily grabbed another swab and pressed it to the woman's face, keeping firm pressure applied as bright red blood leaked over her hand. When Emily glanced up to Lewis in the bed, she could see the horror on his face. She held his gaze for a few seconds and then she spoke clearly. 'She is poorly, Lewis, I need you to tell me everything that you know about her.'

To his credit, Lewis didn't hesitate. 'Her name is Lydia Cox, she is twenty-three years old and she lives in Ealing. As far as I know she has never had any bad health apart from the usual fevers and she has no family except one brother who is still away in France… The child is called Jane and she is three or four years old, something like that… I think she's three.'

He doesn't even know how old his own daughter is.

A grey-haired porter arrived with a stretcher now and they set about moving Lydia up off the floor. It was clear to see that even in this short space of time, her condition was deteriorating; already there was a shadow of blue on her lips. The little girl's face was terrified.

'Come on, sweetie, you come with me,' Alma said as the porter took one end of the stretcher and Emily took the other. Sister had the bed in the side room turned down and ready and waiting. Emily saw her eyes soften as they came in through the door. 'We'll keep the little one here, for the time being, but then she'll have to go up to children's ward. Nurse Burdon, are you all right to stay? And Nurse Adams, you need to make sure the child is settled before you come back onto the ward – we can manage for the time being.'

Alma nodded and reached an arm around the girl. 'Now, you sit right there, on this chair, will you sweetie, while me and the other nurse make your mommy more comfortable in bed?'

The little girl nodded, tears still pouring down her face, but she was calmer now.

Emily and Alma exchanged a wide-eyed glance over the bed as they stripped off the woman's coat and then loosened her white fitted blouse. Lydia's chest was rising and falling rapidly and when Emily picked up her wrist to check her pulse, it was racing. Slipping a mercury thermometer under her patient's arm, Emily went to the bottom of the bed to remove her black leather shoes – they were tatty and the soles were worn thin. Emily grasped her small feet, one at a time, holding each gently just for a moment. Despite her frustration, she felt so sad, knowing that the woman must have struggled to manage. Who knew if Lewis ever sent money for the child? As soon as the thermometer was removed, showing a high fever as expected, Emily asked for Alma's assistance again so that she could prop Lydia high in the bed. They plumped up her pillows and arranged them in a triangular formation, with the softest providing support for her head. Once they were satisfied that she was in the best possible position to assist her breathing, Emily took a moment to smooth back a lock of hair that had fallen onto Lydia's forehead, her hand trembled. She couldn't hide her horror at the high-pitched wheeze that now emanated from Lydia's chest and the tinge of blood that was showing in the white froth from her mouth.

The moment was broken by a whimper from the child who was curled up on the chair. Alma pulled her gently onto her knee, wrapping her in a spare blanket and quietly soothing with her voice. Emily turned from the bed and resolutely took up the flannel that was soaking in a bowl of tepid water that Sister had prepared. Once it was wrung out, she gently sponged Lydia's face, smoothing back the tendrils of black hair from her face. Her mouth was frothing again so she cleaned it carefully, and then she saw the woman open her eyes and try to speak.

'Where is my daughter?'

Emily wrenched down her mask. 'She's here, Lydia, right by you, we will look after her.'

She saw the woman try to smile and she reached out a hand. Emily clasped it with both of her own, smiling back. 'You are safe, we are going to do all that we can to help you,' Emily said, blinking back tears.

Lydia closed her eyes, and just for a moment Emily saw a look of peace on her face, until she began another bout of heaving, crackling breaths. The door opened and James came in. 'Sister asked me to see the visitor who collapsed – the woman who was visiting Sergeant Dupree?' He too was shocked by the turn of events, and she didn't care now whether or not he let it slip that he knew about Lewis and her situation; none of it mattered any more.

James moved his stethoscope around the woman's chest, listening through her spotless white petticoat. When he was done, she saw his brow crease in a frown. 'Both lungs are affected,' he said steadily, shaking his head. Even though it was the news that she was expecting, Emily felt it like a punch and she saw Alma pull the little girl closer.

'Let's keep them both together in here…' he added. 'I know Sister said to send the girl up to children's ward, but I think we can do that after, don't you?'

'But won't she be afraid?' Alma whispered over the head of the child who was now looking very sleepy.

'I think it will be all right,' said Emily, 'In the village where I come from, most people, young and old, they are nursed at home. And if things get bad, well, the children are there too in the house.'

'It's a similar thing on Prince Edward Island,' James said. 'When I was newly qualified, I did a stint near my own family farm. In the spring of that year, we had a spate of mothers dying from childbed fever – they were always nursed at home, with their children right there, aware of what was going on.'

'Yes, but we're strangers to this little girl, we aren't her family…'

'That's true,' offered James, 'but I think this is a better option than sending her off to children's and, don't forget, her father is here on the ward.' He glanced again at Emily. 'I'm not sure how well she knows him though, he's been away to war.'

Alma adjusted the girl's position on her lap and then she used a gentle hand to smooth back the hair from her face. 'I'm still not sure… but I suppose it is the best option that we have right now.'

James nodded and then he spoke decisively. 'Right, I need to get over to female medical, we've had a number of admissions – all flu cases – so I'll be there. But first I'll see Sister and ask if we can get a mattress in here, so the girl can sleep, at least for a while.'

Emily turned her full attention back to her patient. Lydia seemed to have lost consciousness, and the whooping sound that she made with every breath was exactly the same as Lucy's, just before the end. Emily couldn't believe how quickly Lydia had deteriorated. All she could do was continue to stand steadfast by the bed, sponging gently, soothing with her voice; as with all the patients who were dying, the nurses were the only family that they had. And in this case, given that Emily also had a connection to Lewis, perhaps the notion of family was all the more real.

Eventually, a porter with trembling hands and a patch over one eye came in with a cot mattress and some bedding and placed it in the corner of the room. 'Poor little mite,' he murmured, when he saw Lydia on the bed and the girl snuggled on Alma's knee. 'Can you manage the little one, nurse?'

Alma nodded as she carried Lydia and laid her down on the makeshift bed.

The porter, one of the many war veterans who worked in the hospital, cleared his throat and took a handkerchief out of his pocket. 'God bless her,' he said, gazing at Jane as she curled up on the mattress. 'I hope she gets some peaceful sleep.'

After he'd left the room, Alma picked up the chair and brought it across for Emily to sit on. She put an arm around Emily's shoulders then, and gave her a squeeze. 'Come out of the door and holler if you need anything,' she said. 'I don't want you leaving her, not for longer than a few seconds.'

After Alma had gone, Emily moved the chair to the other side of the bed so that she could also keep an eye on the sleeping girl. She wanted to make sure that the child didn't get up and wander out of the door, above the noise of Lydia's breathing and the inevitable paroxysms of coughing that would come, she needed to make extra sure that the child was safe.

Soon, there was more blood mixed with the frothy white secretions from Lydia's mouth and her lips and fingertips were dark blue. She tried to sit up, her eyes opened for just a moment and then her whole body seemed to go rigid; she was still trying to breathe but her chest seemed stuck. Lydia sucked in one more breath and then more blood came from her mouth and her head fell to the side. Her chest was still and silent.

Emily was stunned. She shot a glance to the mattress on the floor where, thankfully, the girl was sleeping peacefully – the gentle rise and fall of her easy breathing was the sweetest sound.

Emily took up the damp cloth once more and wiped around Lydia's face, cleaning as well as she could with the now cold water. She removed some of the pillows to lay the woman's body flat, straightening the limbs. There was no more that she could do right now; they would perform the last rites properly, just as soon as they could.

She heard the little girl murmur in her sleep, and stir. Immediately, Emily took off her mask and white gown, folding them together and pushing them beside the wash bowl. She went to the cold tap in the corner of the room and scrubbed her hands hard with carbolic soap, feeling the sting of it on her dry, cracked skin.

'Mummy, mummy?' the little girl was calling.

Emily grabbed a towel and quickly dried her hands, taking a deep breath as she walked carefully towards the mattress where the girl was sitting up with her hair tousled and her face still scrunched from sleep.

She knelt by the side of the mattress. 'Hello,' she said, making her voice light. 'My name is Emily and I'm a nurse.'

The little girl looked up at her and she rubbed her still sleepy eyes with both hands. 'Where's mummy?' she asked.

Emily opened her mouth to speak. She had never done this before – *how do you tell a small child that her mummy has just died?*

'Well, you remember how poorly mummy was, when you came to the hospital today?'

The girl looked at her with wide eyes. 'Where is mummy? I want mummy…'

Emily put her arms around her then and picked her up. 'Mummy?' called the girl, as soon as she saw her mother on the bed. She was reaching out now, wanting to go to her. It didn't feel like Emily had any other choice than to put her down on the bed, right next to her.

She watched as Jane placed her small hand on Lydia's face. 'Mummy, wake up,' she said. Then when her mummy didn't respond, she reached up and tried to open her eyes. 'Open your eyes Mummy, I want to look at you.' Jane was stroking her face again and when there was no response, she placed her small tousled head on Lydia's chest and just lay there quietly with tears running down her face.

Emily had never seen anything as heart-rending as this, but she didn't want Jane to pick up on any shift of emotion. All she could do now was stand by and make sure that the child was safe as she did what she needed to do.

The door opened quietly behind her and James was there, tears springing to his eyes at the scene before him. He came to stand close beside her, neither of them daring speak. He took her hand gently in his own and Emily felt grateful.

They watched as the girl sat up again and once more tried to open her mummy's eyes. 'Mummy won't wake up,' she said, turning to look at them.

'Your mummy has gone,' James whispered.

'Where has she gone?'

'She's gone to heaven,' he said matter-of-factly.

'I want to go too,' she said, her voice starting to break.

'Well, one day you will go, but not just yet.'

'I want to go now,' she said, scrabbling around on the bed, her face starting to scrunch with fury.

'Do you like candy?' James said, pulling a paper bag of jelly beans out of his pocket, opening it up and holding it out at arm's length. 'These are my favourite.'

The girl stopped, looking from James to Emily and then back again. She frowned and looked away.

'Go on, just try one, they're delicious. My family sent them for me, all the way from Canada.' When Lydia looked again at James, she reached out a hand and took one, peering at if for a few seconds before popping it into her mouth, gazing at them both as she munched it. Then she took another and another, until sticky juice was running down her chin. 'You can have the bag if you want,' he said and she did so, readily.

'Will you come to me, Jane?' said Emily, smiling, and she could have sobbed when the girl reached out her arms and latched right onto her. Feeling the warmth of the child's body and the smell of her hair, she closed her eyes and breathed her in.

'Say goodbye to mummy,' Emily said and Jane waved, 'Bye bye, mummy, bye bye.'

Emily shifted the child's position in her arms. 'Right, let's go and see what we can find,' she said, moving slowly, easing the child away from her mother's bedside.

'I'll make sure that they take this mattress back up to children's ward for her,' said James softly, 'and I'll ask the nurses who lay her out to keep her mother's petticoat, so that the girl can have it in her bed.'

Emily nodded. 'Now, Jane,' she said, 'I'm going to take you up to the ward with all of the other children.'

It was only when she walked out of the door and glanced down the ward to the beds on either side, that she remembered that she'd have to break the news to Lewis.

CHAPTER 15

Emily knew, without a shadow of a doubt, that she wasn't a hard-hearted person, but when she stood by Lewis's bed watching him cry, she truly didn't feel sorry for him at all. In fact, his blubbering made her feel angry – he hadn't asked once how little Jane was or where she was, all that consumed him was his own sense of loss.

He reached out a hand to her but she couldn't take it – how could he imagine that she would comfort him? Two days ago she didn't even know about his relationship with Lydia.

'I'm sorry…' he was saying now, his hand clutching on air.

'Lewis… The child… she will miss her mummy terribly, what are you going to do about her?'

He looked at her as if it had all just occurred to him. 'Jane…' he said, as if it was enough to say her name.

'She's gone up to children's ward now and they've said that they'll be able to keep her there until you're strong enough to take her home.'

'No,' he said, his eyes frantic, 'no, *I* can't have her.'

'What do you mean, you can't have her…? *She is your daughter.*' Emily was struggling to keep her voice down and she saw Sister give her a glance as she walked by the bottom of the bed.

'How can I? I don't even know what I'm going to be doing? And then you and I will be getting married…'

Emily was livid. The pain that she'd pushed down as she'd nursed Lydia and dealt with Jane expanded inside of her now, she felt like she could burst. How could he think, just like that, that they could carry on and get married? When the mother of his child had just passed away and still lay in the side room, waiting to go to the mortuary.

'I didn't know she was going to get sick,' he said, his eyes hard now and his mouth twisted.

'Maybe not, Lewis, but you sure as hell didn't help, bringing her here to visit you on a ward full of flu cases.'

'I had no idea she would come, I didn't even tell her that I was back in London just in case she—'

'Just in case she came here and saw me.'

He looked shame-faced now and when he tried to speak, he stumbled on his words. 'I can't have the girl though, I just can't… She'll have to go to an orphanage.'

Emily saw the little girl's sweet face, the way she'd cried for her mummy. She felt a rush of blood surge through her body and the words exploded out of her, almost in a shout. 'She is not going to an orphanage! If you don't want her, well, I'll… *I'll take her.*'

He turned his face away from her. As weak as he was, she just wanted to grab him, shake him, but she knew no matter what, he wouldn't change his mind.

Sister's heels sounded on the wooden floor. Emily hoped what she'd said had been drowned out by the noise of the ward, but Sister definitely knew that something was up.

'Nurse Burdon?' Sister said, gesturing for her to follow to the bottom of the ward. When she spoke again her voice was full of sympathy. 'You looked agitated with that patient, I know you've just been delivering bad news, but I'm thinking that you need to take some time off the ward. It must have been very difficult for you, dealing with Miss Cox and her child – even the nurses who went in to lay her out were in tears. Nurse Adams, you walk with her back to the nurses' home, will you?'

'No, please, I can manage.'

Sister narrowed her eyes and scrutinised Emily's face. After a meaningful pause, she nodded her consent and then strode away. Emily linked Alma's arm. 'I need to tell you something.' She spoke quickly so that she could get it all said. 'I've been meaning to tell you for ages… That patient Lewis Dupree is – *was* – my fiancé and I had no idea that he was also seeing Lydia and that he had a child with her.'

'What?' Alma gasped. 'Does anybody else know about this?'

'Only James… I had to tell him when I asked if he could arrange transfer for Lewis from the hospital in Dunkirk.'

'Well, I thought I was unshockable but you have certainly surprised me today,' she said. 'You are quite something, Emily Burdon, keeping all of this to yourself.'

Emily took in a breath. 'And the thing is, I can't be with Lewis any more, not now, I can't even stand to look at him.'

'No wonder you feel that way, sweetie, any woman would be the same.'

Emily was shaking her head. 'I feel so strongly about this right now, I want to sever all ties with him. Now. Instantly. There's only one thing stopping me doing that… I've just told Lewis that if he doesn't want Jane, then I will take her.'

'Wow… Well, maybe you were being a little hasty on that score, getting carried away—'

'No. I meant it,' said Emily outright.

For once, Alma seemed to be completely stuck for words.

Later on as she walked beside Alma on their way off the ward, she was still riding high on her decision. She felt lighter, like she could breathe, and she held her head high as she made her way along the corridor. Taking charge of the situation suited her, and when she'd made that promise to Lydia that she would take care of Jane, she'd meant every word of it.

She was already running it through her mind. There was only one way that it could work – she would have to take Jane home to her family just for a few weeks, to allow space to work out exactly what she was going to do. She didn't care about Lewis, he could go and find someone else if he wanted. In fact, she would probably be relieved if he did. All that mattered was that Jane was safe. They'd need the money, so she'd have to work, and she couldn't even contemplate leaving the Marylebone, moving away from London. In her head, she would be coming back and finding somewhere for her and Jane to live, sourcing a kindly childminder... she could make things work.

She would speak to them on children's – they'd already said that they'd keep Jane until Lewis was ready to be discharged – so she could carry on working, and then hopefully the flu cases would fall and she could take some time off to go home, taking Jane with her. She didn't want to write and tell them about the situation, especially given that Lewis's family also lived in the village; it would be best to deal with it when she got there. She felt quite satisfied with her plan.

Back on duty the next day, things didn't seem quite so clear cut. As soon as she arrived on the ward, she saw Lewis turn his head and he smiled in her direction. *What's he up to?* she thought, feeling Alma squeeze her hand.

Later on, when she was passing his bed, he called out and she had no choice but to go over to him. 'I've been thinking about what you said,' he announced, running a hand through his untidy hair, 'and I've decided that I can take the girl after all. She's a bonny little thing and when we are married, well, she'll just blend in with the family.'

Emily was aghast, had he always been so flippant and she'd just never realised, or had the war changed him so much that he was like a complete stranger to her now? She was about to say that they wouldn't be getting married now, but as she opened her mouth, something struck her. Jane was Lewis's daughter, and he would have the final say in whatever happened to her. Instantly, she knew that she had to be careful if she was going to have any influence over what would become of the child; she would have to play Lewis at his own game. She still knew enough of him to be able to do that.

'You're still not better, Lewis,' she said, making her voice gentle. 'I don't think you should be committing yourself just yet, let's see how you feel in a few weeks' time. They're happy to keep Jane on children's ward until you're ready. I might be able to get some time off, maybe we could go back home together when you're well?'

'Yes, you're right,' he said, reaching for her hand. 'And this time, there's no choice. If I've got the girl, I'll have to go back to the village.'

Emily stepped back. All the times that she'd been desperate for him to come home with her, but now everything was different and she wasn't sure how to feel. 'Just one thing though, Sister doesn't know about our situation and she thought that Lydia was your fiancée, so it might be best if we keep strictly to nurse and patient relations, whilst you're on the ward.'

'Understood.' Lewis gave her a small salute. 'And just to let you know, I had word from Lydia's brother today. He's her only next of kin, and they sent him a telegram from the hospital. He's still in France, but coming back to make the funeral arrangements and sort out her affairs.'

'Oh, that's good…' But inside, Emily felt for the poor young woman who Lewis had grieved for yesterday but now seemed to be speaking of so easily, as if he'd hardly known her at all.

*

As the weeks slipped by, Emily kept up a strict routine of working on the ward and being civil to Lewis and visiting Jane whenever she could. She'd seen Lydia's brother come in to speak to Lewis – a handsome man with dark curly hair just like his sister's. Emily had liked him; he had a gentle way about him. Lewis had been able to persuade him that he would take good care of his niece, and that he was welcome to come and visit her whenever he wanted.

Emily was becoming increasingly close to Jane. She was such a bright little thing, and all of the nurses loved her. Emily had spotted Lydia's petticoat in Jane's cot – the nurses said that the child slept with it tucked around her and that she woke up at night crying for her mummy. But at three years old she was playful and easy to distract during the day. One day a plush teddy bear appeared, brought in by Dr Cantor. Emily smiled and picked up the teddy, moving its jointed arms and legs, gazing at its glassy brown eyes and slightly lopsided mouth – it seemed to have its own character.

'Teddy,' said Jane, reaching her arms up for the toy.

'She loves it,' said one of the nurses in passing, 'she carries it with her everywhere, and if she's been wandering around the ward and she loses it, she's inconsolable until we find it.'

Well, thought Emily, *no surprise really, James was there right from the start of her new life.* She felt a prickle of sensation when she thought about him and how he'd held her hand when they'd stood by Lydia's bed. It was no more than any of her other colleagues would have done, she told herself. And nothing like what she'd seen between him and Alma that evening at the back of the hospital. Alma had never mentioned a word about it, and that seemed strange; she was always ready to discuss any number of her romances, so why not talk about James? Emily would never have confronted her; she didn't want Alma to think that she'd been snooping. And given the current issues that they were dealing with on a daily basis at the hospital, it all faded into insignificance. Even so, Emily couldn't deny that the knowledge of it was like a piece of grit rubbing away at her friendship with Alma, stopping them from having a true closeness.

*

As Christmas approached, thankfully the number of flu cases admitted began to fall and life on the wards began to take on some semblance of normality. At last, one or two of the nurses had been able to take leave from the ward and Sister had even started talking of making some paper chains to decorate the hospital for Christmas. Lewis was up and about now and getting stronger every day; he'd managed to charm Sister Montgomery and she allowed him free rein for visiting Jane on the children's ward. It felt like the time was right to be asking for some time away – Emily had already hinted to Sister that she lived in the same village as Lewis and that if she took some leave they could both travel back together so that she could make sure that he and Jane arrived home safely.

Given Sister's soft spot for Lewis and the general affection for the motherless little girl that permeated the whole hospital, Sister was ready to agree, and arrangements were made. A week before Christmas, as the nurses were erecting colourful paper chains throughout a hospital that still echoed with the ravages of a disease that had swept through and left them all reeling, Emily was packing her suitcase and saying a tearful goodbye to Grace and Alma.

She'd written to her parents and Lewis had told her that he'd informed his mother, but neither of them had mentioned anything about Jane – it had seemed the best way, so that they could answer any questions in person. It had been easy to keep her thoughts about Lewis under control; she'd almost begun to think of him as just another patient on the ward. After all, he presented well and Sister Montgomery had established a good rapport with him. When it suited him, he could be ever so charming. She'd managed to distance herself so much from him that she'd stood and listened calmly as he told her how he'd met

Lydia on a train when he was coming home on leave that first time and he had nowhere to stay, when Emily was working and couldn't get time away.

She hadn't taken on too much of his version of what happened next. She knew him well enough now to realise how good he was at spinning a yarn, how he could worm his way out of most things... There were flashes of the old Lewis still there, but when he thought no one was looking, she could see that hardened look on his face, his eyes empty. She couldn't be sure how things would go, but despite everything, she was telling herself that she needed to give him a chance if they were to do what was best for Jane.

The pale early morning light was just starting to break through the Infirmary windows as they walked along the corridor on the day of departure. Lewis up ahead, still slightly out of breath, with the new suit that he'd got one of the porters to buy for him loose around him and his army pack on his back. Emily had been a little shocked to see how handsome he looked after the ward barber had cut his hair and he'd donned a new white shirt. He was still thin but she could see the man he used to be again, not just the patient lying in a bed. As she followed along behind him, carrying a sleepy Jane with Teddy tucked beneath her arm, she shivered in the cold air. There were feathers of ice on the inside of the windows and Emily was glad of the warmth of the child nestled against her.

Hearing the sound of feet behind and a familiar voice calling her name, Emily turned to see Alma running along the corridor, holding her cap in place with one hand. 'I know we said our goodbyes last night, Emily,' she said, bending over slightly to catch her breath, 'but Sister allowed me off the ward for five minutes to see you again. She sends her best wishes and I just wanted to remind you to write, please write.'

Emily felt the softness of Alma's skin and the smell of her expensive soap as she put her arms around Emily and Jane in one big embrace. There were tears shining in Alma's eyes.

'I'll be back in the new year,' Emily reassured.

Alma stepped back, blinking. 'I don't know if you will. I just have a feeling about this... seeing how you are with Jane...'

Alma was saying out loud something that Emily had been trying to bury, something that she knew might well be the case. 'We'll see... But please don't worry, Alma, I will write to you. And I hope you have a good Christmas, we've always had a party on the ward. I'm not sure about this year, but I hope that there will be something going on.'

'We'll do our best, don't worry. Sister has already been thinking about small presents for the patients, and some kind of Christmas dinner.'

Emily smiled. She knew how kind-hearted Sister Montgomery was at Christmas and how obsessed about the coloured paper chains. And she always made sure they had a good supply of crackers and a tree for the ward. Emily would miss it, she'd even miss all of those hours spent together in the common room after work, making decorations. She'd always loved the warmth of the pre-Christmas activities, especially with Lucy by her side.

'I'd best go,' Emily said, 'the taxi cab will be waiting.' Leaning in, she gave Alma a kiss on the cheek.

'Oh and there's this,' Alma laughed, revealing a bag of jelly beans for Jane and a letter for Emily. 'James said he's been trying to see you to say goodbye, but he's been so busy...'

'Oh, right, thank you...' Emily replied, feeling a little disconcerted. She'd seen him a number of times in passing in the corridor over the last week and he'd always nodded a quick hello. She wondered why he hadn't taken a few minutes to speak to her, if he was so concerned.

'Send him my best wishes!' she called as Alma turned away. Emily glanced back once more to see her fast disappearing down the corridor, the sound of her shoes echoing in the tiled corridor.

'Safe journey!' Alma called, from a distance. 'And Merry Christmas!'

She caught what sounded like a mournful note in her friend's voice. It made leaving even harder than it already was. She adjusted Jane's weight on her hip, leaning a cheek against her curly head, just for a moment. 'Come on then sweetie, let's go,' she murmured, just as she heard Lewis's voice calling impatiently that if they didn't get a move on they'd miss their train.

CHAPTER 16

The northbound train was crowded and Emily and Jane were separated from Lewis – she was glad, she didn't really want to get into too much conversation with him, not yet at least. Over the weeks since Lydia had died, she'd made sure to keep a distance, striving at all times to treat him just like any other patient. It hadn't been easy at first but as time passed it had almost become second nature. Although Lewis had abided by the rules and played his part, she knew him well enough to be aware that he wasn't happy with the arrangement and he'd often become impatient if she was at another bed, always wanting his own needs to be her priority. She'd stayed calm, smoothing over his disgruntled comments, not wanting to get into anything that could spiral out of control. But now, once he was up and dressed and they were on their way out of the hospital, she'd seen the hungry look that he was giving her and it sent a shiver of anxiety down her spine.

The nurses on the children's ward had cried when they'd had to say goodbye to Jane – they'd really taken to her and they'd brought her through the worst of the night terrors and the moments when she'd begged for her mummy. Emily knew that Jane wasn't over it yet – perhaps she never would be – but the little girl who the nurses had handed over, complete with a thick winter coat and a woolly hat, scarf and gloves knitted by one of the night nurses, was the best that she possibly could be, given the circumstances. They'd even provided wax crayons and a pad, some small wooden farm animals and a reading book for the journey. These items, plus the jelly beans from James, helped to get Jane settled on the train.

In no time, the little girl was snuggled up with Emily's arm around her, drawing her small body close. Although Emily had visited children's as often as she could, she hadn't been able to spend long periods of time with Jane, so she was at first intrigued by the number of questions that the little girl asked. She'd answered every single one as carefully as she could for the first couple of hours, but then she'd had to try and distract her instead – Emily's head was buzzing with having to think up answers to *How does the train move? Why is that man with the funny hat asking for tickets? What makes a red crayon red?*

Relieved to see Jane starting to yawn and look sleepy, Emily adjusted her into a more comfortable position and stared out of the window at the passing landscape. She'd lost track of where they were now, but she watched the fields and trees go by as the train puffed along, clouds of steam swirling at either side. A chestnut horse snorted and then took off at a gallop, racing across a field, startled by the sound of the iron engine moving at speed. Emily almost cried out with joy when she saw the free movement of the beautiful creature.

Jane was breathing more heavily now and when Emily peeked at her, her eyes were shut tight. She leaned back against the seat, starting to relax. She didn't want to drift off to sleep herself, just in case the girl woke up, but seeing the kindly middle-aged woman who sat with her knitting in the opposite seat, Emily knew that Jane probably wouldn't come to much harm even if she did. The woman had smiled at Emily a few times and she'd said, *Your daughter is so beautiful.* Emily didn't correct her – she didn't want to go into any of the detail, so she'd smiled back and said, *Thank you.*

She thought about Lydia then and she renewed her pledge. *I will always remember that she was yours and she will always know about you. I will do my best to look after her.* It had become a mantra over the last few weeks, something that had made it easier for her to leave the work that she loved. As she sat now with Jane snuggled against her, her eyelids blue-veined and almost transparent, her soft hair falling in corkscrew curls, Emily already knew that she adored her.

Thinking about leaving work reminded Emily of the letter from James that she'd shoved in her pocket. She rooted it out and managed to peel it open with one hand. Once she had it out of the envelope, she gave it a firm shake so that it opened fully. She felt a tingle go through her when she saw the bold flourish of his handwriting – it really was impressive. She was expecting this to be a routine *Goodbye, hope you have a good Christmas, we will miss you*, but as she read beyond *Dear Emily*, she felt a warm flush at the base of her throat.

> *I know you must have felt it strange that I haven't been to see you in the last few weeks but I've been finding it hard. Even passing you in the corridor has made me too flustered to be able to speak. I'm sorry if it has upset you or made me seem rude, but the truth is, Emily, my feelings for you have become strong, almost too strong for me to manage. I know that this might come as a shock, mostly we just go along in our work, putting all else aside, and, normally, I would never have made my feelings known. But the experience of these last weeks and months, seeing young men and women in the prime of their lives struck down by this terrible flu, has made me think differently. Our work in the medical profession makes us all too aware of how fragile life can be and how it can be cut short so abruptly, and that is why I am writing. Life is for living, Emily, and there is much to be said for making one's feelings known. So, here goes… I fell for you on that first day – when I saw you in*

the corridor with your friend and noted that streak of red in your hair. You probably won't believe me, but it is true. The more we worked together, the more my feelings grew, and although this all seems impossible, I just need you to know that you are very special and I will never forget you.

I understand, of course, that your situation is complicated, you are still engaged to Lewis and now you have the care of Jane. I can only respect you for that and respect your wishes. If you want to cut contact with me, now that I have declared my feelings, I will understand, but I will not give up all hope, not yet at least.

I hope you enjoy the time with your family and have a good Christmas.

Ever yours,
James

Emily's mouth dropped open as she read the letter and when she looked up, the woman opposite gave her a concerned glance as you would to someone who'd had bad news. Emily smiled to put the woman at her ease, before reading the letter again, every tiny detail of the last few months running through her mind. She was flabbergasted; could this be true? They'd all been overworked and overwrought, maybe he'd started to unravel? But it sounded so measured, so well thought-out and so beautifully written that she knew it had to be, and it made her ache with longing.

Letting the letter rest in her lap, she gazed out of the window again. She knew that she had feelings for James; yes, she'd tried to deny them, but she'd always had them. Then again, so did half the women at the Infirmary. And what about Alma? She was sure of what she'd seen out there at the back of the hospital, only weeks ago. That in itself was enough to warn Emily off – and added to the experience that she'd had with Lewis's infidelity… well, could she handle any further complications – or heartbreak – in her life? Outside of work, she knew nothing about James. What if he was a Lewis, collecting women's hearts wherever he went?

Sighing, she slipped the letter back inside the envelope, she had no idea what she was going to do about this. She no longer felt that she owed much to Lewis, but it was impossible to escape the memory of him. When she'd seen him dressed in his suit, it had brought him back to her with a jolt. They'd grown up together; she would never be able to replace that first kiss they'd shared one summer as the sun was setting. It had been hay time, the ground had been warm and the sweet smell of cut grass hung in the air. They'd been walking arm in arm, laughing together about something, when he'd stopped and turned to her. The kiss was unexpected, tender, and completely innocent. And just for that moment, aged sixteen, she'd felt as if they breathed the same breath. Thinking about it even now, even after all these years, gave her a sentimental glow that made her heart ache.

The train gave a jolt and Emily was back to the present, with the warmth of the child's body nestled against her, and instantly she recalled how Lewis's mouth had twisted when he'd said that his daughter should go to an orphanage. Almost as if Jane could feel her thoughts, the girl scrunched her face and made as if to cry in her sleep. Emily drew her closer. Right now, wanting to care for Jane was the only thing that seemed clear to her.

The sound of a hacking cough in the next compartment sent a stab of alarm right through her body and almost as if it was a nervous reaction, she felt a tickle in her own throat and she began to cough. She heard an intake of breath around the compartment and slapped a hand across her mouth, immediately rooting with one hand for the cotton mask that she carried in her bag. Not able to tie it without disturbing Jane, she held it across her nose and mouth, forcing herself to swallow and take a succession of deep, steady breaths. She'd never felt like this in the hospital, even in a ward full of flu patients. Seeing the woman opposite looking over her wire-rimmed spectacles and blinking uncertainly, Emily assured her that it was a mere tickle, not a flu symptom.

Some time later, Lewis stumbled against the window of their compartment. She raised a hand to acknowledge him but prayed that he wouldn't open the door – he looked like he'd had a good few swigs from that silver flask she'd seen him slip inside his jacket pocket. After everything he'd been through in France and then in the hospital, Emily didn't want to judge, but she hated to imagine if he'd been in sole charge of Jane. When he raised a hand and moved along, she breathed out a sigh of relief.

Stepping down from the train with her suitcase in one hand and Jane holding tight to the other, she was surprised to see Lewis waiting with a smile and reaching out immediately to take her bag. He seemed to have sobered up and, once again, she saw a glimmer of the old Lewis in that smile, the Lewis who she'd seen off from this very station at the start of the war.

Every time she'd been through here since, on her visits home, she'd thought about that day. All the wives and mothers and girlfriends crammed on the platform, waving and crying. Some, like her, crushing to the front to stand on tiptoe as steam coiled around them, reaching up to the open windows for one final kiss even as the train started to pull away.

She would never forget the cheers and the swell of emotion that ran through the crowd. Some of the men, awkward and full of bravado in their new uniforms, had been leaning out and shouting or laughing, others stood silently at the windows with solemn faces. The hard press of Lewis's kiss that day had left her dizzy and she'd staggered away, glad of her eldest sister, Alice's steady arm – she'd also been saying her own stoic goodbyes to her long-term boyfriend, Harold. Sadly, Harold had been shot dead at the Somme, caught by a bullet as he was going over the top. Alice had never been one to share her feelings and she seemed to have taken the news as stoically as she'd said her goodbye, but who knew what she'd been feeling underneath? It had made Emily feel a bit guilty, to still have Lewis alive.

These thoughts of the past softened Emily's feelings and she took Lewis's arm as they pushed their way through the crowd. They looked like a family, just one couple amongst many, under the high roof of the railway station. Coming out onto the road, she heard the excitement in Lewis's voice as he called to his friend, Stan, who'd agreed to give them a lift home in his delivery van. Stan was from the next village and Emily didn't know him well, but he gave her a cheery wave before grabbing Lewis around the shoulders and giving him a rough squeeze. They'd both joined up at the same time, at the start of the war, but Stan had been pensioned off early after suffering a bad wound to his leg. He walked now with a marked limp but it didn't seem to hold him back as he moved around the van, opening up the back doors. 'Women and children first!' He laughed, indicating a nest of blankets on the floor. Emily scrambled in with Jane as Lewis went up front to sit next to Stan.

She could hear them laughing uproariously as the solid tyres of the vehicle bumped over the cobbles outside the station and then along the main road that led to the narrow country roads. It was pitch black outside once they'd left the street lights behind, so she had to gauge where they were by the sound of the tyres on the road and the branches that scraped the sides of the van once they were out on the country roads – it wouldn't be long now before they were home. As they bumped along with the child tucked in beside her, Emily realised that it had perhaps been a bit strange that Stan hadn't passed any comment about Jane. She hadn't heard Lewis say anything to him, so why didn't he at least ask who the little girl was? At first she put it down to being a man, but then her heart clenched when the realisation came that Stan had probably known about Lydia and Jane all along. She pulled Jane closer, feeling unsettled now when she heard both men laughing on and off and talking non-stop and by the tone of Lewis's voice, she was pretty sure that they were drinking.

She just hoped that once they were home, Lewis didn't start spending all of his time in the pub like he had the last time he'd been back. It wasn't the fact that she'd hardly see him that worried her, it was knowing what too much drink did to him, and especially now that she had Jane, she didn't want him scaring her. Thankfully, he'd readily agreed that Jane should go along to stay at Emily's parents' house and not his. He would be dreading confronting his father, and there was always trouble when he came home. Lewis had said himself that it was no place for a child.

When the van finally lurched to a halt Emily felt a surge of longing. It had been ages since she'd seen her family and she couldn't wait to be back in through the door of their home.

'Come on,' she said to Jane, standing up as well as she could in the confines of the van. She could hear the two men opening their doors and jumping down; it would only be moments before they were released. She waited a bit longer; she could hear their voices still, and then Stan's laugh.

'Won't be long,' she murmured to Jane, but it was dark in the back and the little girl started to whimper. Something snapped inside her then and she twisted round, banging on the side of the van. There was no response, though she could still hear them. She shouted for Lewis, infuriated when all she could hear was the sound of his laughter. That was it. She kept her voice calm so as not to frighten Jane, but she went to the doors and hammered on them, loud enough for anyone to hear.

'All right, all right,' Stan was saying as he swung open the back doors. 'You've got a feisty one here, Lewis.'

Emily felt the night air strike cold on her face as she jumped straight down and turned to take Jane in her arms. Reaching in to retrieve her own suitcase, she walked away with Jane settled on her hip. She heard Stan whistle between his teeth and make some comment, which was followed by Lewis's laughter. She was seething, but she just kept on walking, not even turning her head to offer a riposte.

Although it was pitch dark, there was some light from the houses that surrounded the village green and she could see the ancient stone cross that stood square in the middle. She walked as quickly as she could, her heart hammering furiously against her ribs. Hearing Jane whimper again, she made herself calm down. The van had stopped outside Lewis's house which adjoined the forge, so Emily needed to walk to the opposite end of the green where their own house stood apart from the rest – a good-sized stone-built property with the shop at the front and living accommodation to the rear and above. Looking at it now, she knew she must leave behind the aggravation with Lewis; she didn't want anything to mar her return home. Some of the villagers scoffed at the Burdons and their happy family, as if that in itself was something to be derided. But her family didn't care, they'd always been at the centre of the village and even after her dad's illness, they'd always been happy.

There were lights on in the church and, as she approached, she heard the sound of an organ – it must be a carol practice and her sisters would be in there with the choir. The old hand-pumped church organ sounded just as wheezy as it always had as it offered some breathy introductory notes, but when the singing began, Emily felt tears springing to her eyes. It was one of her favourite carols, 'Oh Holy Night'. Irresistibly, she was singing along, her breath catching when she came to the line, 'Fall on your knees, Oh hear the angel voices!' She had to stop for a moment and turn back to gaze at the stained-glass windows of the church; the coloured light was flooding out onto the cold ground. She felt Jane put her arms around her neck and snuggle closer. Emily whispered some sweet nonsense in her ear and felt the low murmur of the girl's laughter. 'I like this song, Mummy,' she said.

Emily's heart jumped a beat. She knew that the girl was just tired and she was saying the oft-repeated word, but it made Emily feel that connection again to Lydia. She gazed up to the sky; the moon was looking down at them and the stars were bright and clear, like diamonds. 'Look, Jane,' she said, 'look at the stars.'

'Is that heaven, up there?' Jane said quietly, pointing with her finger.

'Yes, it is,' Emily replied, giving her a kiss on the cheek. 'That's where your mummy is.'

Emily walked past the front of the house, noting a large advertisement pinned up in the shop window for Veno's lightning cough cure. *Spanish flu, many deaths prevented*, it promised. She felt a stab of anger. It didn't seem right for anyone to be laying claim to something like that; there was nothing that could hold back the disease. She would speak to Alice and Lizzie tomorrow, ask them to take the poster down.

As soon as she saw the deep green paint of the back door, she began to smile. Putting her case down on the back step, she tapped on the door before opening it – sometimes her mother dozed off in the chair and Emily didn't want to startle her. Hearing no sound, she opened the door wider and slipped Jane down to stand on the flagstones, whilst she retrieved her suitcase. As they walked through into the warm kitchen, Jane held tightly to her hand. The stove was still lit and the little girl gave a small exclamation of delight when she saw the marmalade tabby cat who always lay there, stretched in front of the fire.

'That's Rusty,' Emily said, 'you can go and stroke him if you want.'

Jane glanced up and smiled and then she was crouching next to the cat, her small hand gently stroking the length of his body.

The cat lifted his head for a moment and looked at her, and then he was stretching out even further as Jane spoke to him quietly, babbling all kinds of jumbled-up stories.

Now that she was inside her childhood home, and she had the girl with her, Emily couldn't help but feel a little nervous. She knew that Jane would be welcomed of course, but she'd have to tell the whole story and that made her stomach clench.

'Hello?' she called, and then she heard a rustle from the sitting room and her mother was coming through the door, crying out, 'Emily, it's Emily!'

Normally she would have run to meet her, but Jane was still sitting on the kitchen floor with her hand resting on the cat. When Maggie Burdon appeared, she didn't see Jane initially and she walked through with her arms open, her face glowing with a huge smile. Then she stopped, drawing in a breath, her dark eyes bright with the inevitable question.

Emily cleared her throat. 'This is Jane,' she said, unable to hide the slight waver in her voice. 'She is Lewis's child.'

Her mother gasped.

Emily walked into her mother's embrace, needing to come straight out with the detail. 'He was involved in a relationship with another woman. She was called Lydia and she died from the flu.'

'Oh, Emily, what a thing for you to have to deal with.' Her mother hugged her extra close and when she stood back Emily saw her wipe her eyes quickly with the back of her hand.

Once they were sitting at the table together with a cup of tea, Emily filled her in on what had happened with Lewis and Lydia. All the while her mother was listening, she was glancing to Jane, still with the cat, telling another story now in a made-up language.

When Emily had finished speaking, all that could be heard was the slow drop of ash from the fire grate and Jane's chirpy voice, lying down now across the stone flags, still in her coat and hat.

Her mother looked up and smiled at Emily, pushing a stray lock of her greying blonde hair behind one ear. 'It's as it is,' she said, matter of fact, 'and the child is welcome here, of course she is.'

Emily breathed out and started taking off her coat as her mother crouched down beside Jane to say hello. 'He's a lazy old thing,' she said, giving the cat a scratch behind the ears.

'Does he like to eat jelly beans?' asked Jane, her eyes wide and her face all serious.

'I don't think so, but he loves sardines.'

Jane nodded, as if she was weighing up the situation.

'Do you want to come with me and we'll find some sardines for him to eat?'

Jane got up, eager to assist, as Maggie started to help her take off her coat.

'This is all going to be fine, Emily, don't you worry, your sisters will be back from choir practice in half an hour and they'll be delighted to meet our new guest. And wait till your father gets up in the morning…' Maggie said, taking Jane's hand to wander off together towards the pantry as if it was the most natural thing in the world.

CHAPTER 17

Emily woke early in her childhood room beside Jane. They'd always been lucky, sleeping above the shop – they had four good-sized bedrooms, one room each for the Burdon sisters. Emily's room was just as she'd left it with the patchwork quilt on the creaky iron-framed bed and the pictures of horses and dogs on the wall. A small, framed photo of Lewis in his uniform – a smaller version of the one she had at the hospital – stood on her bedside table.

It was the first thing she saw when she turned from checking on Jane as soon as she woke. There he was again with that bright smile, so handsome in his uniform. She took the photo in her hand and looked at it more closely. It still made her heart sink to note the change in him. With a sigh, she reached over and slipped it into the top drawer of her bedside table with all the bric-a-brac she'd left behind. She'd always meant to sort the drawer out; the photo now lay on top of hair pins and spools of embroidery thread, a small tin that had contained mints, and a penny whistle that she'd saved from a long-ago Christmas cracker.

Jane had been fast asleep by the time Alice and Lizzie came through the door the night before, still singing carols and both red-cheeked from the cold and looking cherubic with their wavy blonde hair and matching knitted hats. They'd listened wide-eyed as she'd told the story, both sneaking up the stairs for a peek at the sleeping child. Alice had cried when she'd seen Jane's little face and her black curls spilling onto the pillow. Lizzie had beamed. 'She's so cute… I hope that Lewis doesn't come and take her away.'

Emily's heart had clenched, even though she'd come straight out and said, 'No, he won't do that.' All she could add further was, 'It's all going to be fine, I'll make sure that it works out.' But she knew that she was far from sure that would be the case. Even on the journey home, her feelings for Lewis had veered back and forth, and the thought of him still wanting to marry her made her feel panicked. She would have to wait and see what happened, now they were both home.

Given the luxury of not needing to get up for work that morning, Emily rolled onto her side and soon fell back to sleep. When she woke up again, Jane was murmuring beside her, talking to her teddy. As soon as Jane saw Emily's face she beamed and Emily felt her heart squeeze tight with happiness.

'Come on, let's go downstairs,' Emily said, helping Jane out of bed, both of them padding down the stairs together in their nighties – it made her feel like a child again.

'I've told your father about the girl,' Maggie said, 'go on in and see him.'

Emily took Jane by the hand and led her through into the sitting room where Charles Burdon had his bed and spent most of his days in the wheelchair. He gave a lopsided smile as they came through the door and Emily could see tears in his eyes.

'This is Jane,' she said, 'and she's going to stay with us for Christmas.'

Charles made a noise in the back of his throat – the damage to his brain had taken his speech, but he still found ways of communicating.

Jane was unconcerned and she went straight up to him and plonked Teddy on his knee. 'Say hello to Teddy.' The little girl smiled. It was a wonderful moment, but Emily worried about how her father might feel – she knew how frustrated he could get when his words wouldn't come. But this time, he gave another of his lopsided smiles and then made a sound, his own approximation of *hello*.

Jane was perfectly happy with that and she continued to chatter on as Charles reached out his one good hand to stroke Teddy's ear, and then as Jane leaned in closer, Emily saw him gently touch her soft curls. The next thing, Jane was indicating that she wanted to scramble up onto his knee. Emily helped her on board and Charles brought his one good arm around the little girl and indicated to Emily that he wanted her to wheel him through to the kitchen.

'Well, look who we've got here!' called Maggie, turning from the stove as they came through the door.

Emily began to feel like a weight was lifting from her as she sat at the breakfast table with her family. Jane perched on a cushion between her two sisters as her mother plied them with porridge and eggs and piles of toast slathered with butter. Realising that she was light-headed with hunger, Emily ate and ate as they all chatted together, catching up as rapidly as they could before Alice and Lizzie needed to don their work aprons and go through to the shop.

As they cleared away the pots, Maggie turned to Emily, her face serious. 'You need to take some time for yourself… What with all this stuff with Lewis – and I can't even imagine how busy you've been at the hospital.'

'It has been bad,' Emily agreed, glancing to Jane, who was playing with some wooden blocks that Lizzie had found and the carved animals that the nurses had given her. 'Especially with Lucy, and then Lewis, getting sick, and then what happened to Lydia…' It all felt so raw, speaking of it now in the warm kitchen. But she couldn't open up fully, not here, so instead, she asked, 'How have things been here, are you still clear of flu in the village?'

'By some miracle, but they've got plenty of cases in town. I mean, I knew when I heard that the Prime Minister had got this,

I said, *if David Lloyd George can get it, then anyone can*. And hasn't it been terrible? We've kept thinking it's bound to come here – and we've all been taking precautions, washing hands, wearing masks if somebody gets a cough. You never see folk spitting in the street, not here at any rate.'

'You're doing all the right things,' Emily said, knowing that there wouldn't have been any point trying to offer meaningless reassurances. 'We just need to stay vigilant.'

Maggie nodded, plunging her hands into the hot soapy water to get the breakfast dishes washed. Emily picked up a tea towel and as she dried, Maggie started to tell her bits and pieces of village news and what she'd prepared for Christmas. 'I'll get a few extra bits and pieces for Jane and we've just had some kaleidoscopes in the shop – I could put one of those in her stocking.'

Christmas Eve came along and by that time the house was decorated with paper chains and a freshly cut tree smelling of rich pine, taking Emily straight back to childhood Christmases. Together, the sisters helped Jane to cover the tree with cotton wool balls and hand-painted ornaments made from wood and papier mâché – each one telling a story of a past Christmas or school project. Meanwhile, Maggie worked hard to make sure that the turkey they had every year was ready for the oven and the pudding was brought down from the shelf. All they needed now was to go out to church for the evening carol service and then come back for a supper of cold meats and blackberry wine.

As they all walked together by the side of the village green, Alice pushing Charles in his wheelchair with Jane on his knee, Emily saw a man staggering towards them. Even in the dark she knew that it was Lewis, and by the look of him, he was very drunk. She'd expected him to turn up at their door every day since they'd been home, but he'd never shown his face. Not really any surprise, given the story that he knew she would have shared with her family. But even so, she thought he might at least have come to see Jane.

Emily fell back behind the rest of the party, knowing that he would probably make a beeline for her and, true to form, he stumbled in her direction. As he got closer, he made a grab for her, clutching her arm and moving his face up close. He reeked of beer. His speech was so slurry that she couldn't make out what he was saying and as she tried to shake free of him, he started shouting and his grip on her upper arm tightened.

She saw Lizzie running back. 'Let go of her, Lewis!' she growled, but he scowled and swore and tried to drag Emily away. Lizzie wasn't having any of it and she was used to dealing with men who turned up drunk in the shop. 'That's enough,' she said, her dark eyes blazing as she took his hand and peeled back his fingers. 'We need you to be going on your way now, please.' Lizzie was small compared to Alice, but she had a way of standing her ground and speaking with authority.

Emily felt Lewis release the pressure on her arm and she was able to break free. When she glanced back, she could see him still swaying. Even though her arm was stinging with pain, she couldn't help but feel sad for him, standing there all alone. It wasn't unusual to see the village men drunk on Christmas Eve – the pub was open and it was always busy. But she'd never seen Lewis as bad as this so early in the evening. It seemed that he hadn't even remembered that he had a daughter.

The single bell of the village church rang out loud and clear for Christmas morning and it was all excitement in the house. The shop was closed for two whole days, giving the family time together, and this year they had Jane. The little girl squealed with delight when she saw that the stocking she'd hung above the fireplace was bulging with goodies and a candy cane was sticking out from the top. There were gifts to unwrap and the cat, Rusty, wove his way between discarded crêpe paper. As the aroma of turkey cooking in the oven mingled with the smell of the tree, this felt like a real Christmas for Emily.

She thought about Alma and Grace at the hospital. They'd still be busy on the wards, nursing flu cases. And then there was James – she'd tried to put him out of her head, she'd really tried, but she'd read and re-read that letter and she still didn't know what to do. He would be missing home; it sounded like that he also had a close family and, like her, he lived in a farming community. He would be missing all of the things that she was now enjoying.

'Emily!' Jane shouted, holding out a cracker for her to pull.

'Bang!' Emily said, when the snap didn't snap, but Jane was already scrabbling on the floor to pick up the small toy that had fallen out.

Later on, after mince pies and glasses of sherry, when her father was dozing in his chair and Jane had gone for her nap, Emily began to feel restless. She'd felt sure that there would have been a tap on the door this morning and that she'd have found Lewis there, bleary eyed and smelling of drink, but still wanting to see his daughter. But there was no sign of him. And as the light began to fade outside, so did Emily's hopes that Jane's father would at least want to make some contact. Not that the little girl had any awareness, despite the number of times he'd visited her on the ward. She hadn't ever been able to distinguish him from James or one of the porters, she had never called him Daddy. But it irked Emily, probably more than it should have; she wanted it for Jane more than anything.

She'd already got her hat and coat on before Maggie spotted that she was about to go out through the door.

'I'm going over to see Lewis,' Emily explained.

She saw both her sisters' heads turn and then they were up out of their seats.

'Do you think that's a good idea, after how he was last night?' said Lizzie.

'Probably not, but what else can I do? It's Christmas and what would it say about the spirit of the whole thing, if I didn't at least try and make some contact with him?'

'I'm coming with you,' said Alice, 'even if I just stand outside, I want to make sure that you're safe.'

'No, honestly, I know that he was a mess last night, but he's probably just letting off steam, and if I know Lewis, he'll be nursing a sore head today and he'll be as quiet as a mouse.'

Emily wasn't entirely sure this would be true – and she didn't dare tell them about the purple bruises that she now had at the top of her arm – but she needed to go out and do this on her own. She'd never been afraid of Lewis and she wouldn't start to be now.

Emily pulled her blue wool coat closely around her body and shoved her gloved hands into her pockets as she stepped out into the cold air, ice already underfoot. She knew that the brook would be solid with ice and tomorrow there would be hordes of children out, sliding and skating. It felt comforting to see the lights on in each of the houses as she made her way around the green, and as she passed the stone cross, she heard a giggle and two young people jumped up and scurried away – it made her smile, she'd often met up with Lewis at that very same spot.

Approaching the forge, she could see that it was in darkness, the one day of the year when there was never a fire glowing red and then white hot. She'd been in there sometimes in winter, when Lewis was still working, when it had been hot enough for him to stand stripped down to the waist, pouring with sweat, whilst she was bound up in a thick coat. She'd never gone near if his father was there – Frank Dupree was a daunting presence, six feet tall and heavily muscled, he was a man of very few words.

As a young blacksmith he'd been kicked so hard by a horse that he'd been shoeing that his arm had been broken. The story was that the creature had never harmed a living soul before and she'd heard folk saying that horses can always sense when somebody's not right. It hadn't made her feel any more relaxed around the man, especially after Lewis had told her some of the things that had happened to him at his father's hands. That's why she was determined to see Lewis now, especially on Christmas Day.

It was almost pitch black as she stood outside his house in a weak halo of light coming through the slit of glass at the top of the door. She knocked once, then a second time when she failed to rouse anyone initially. Someone was coming to the door now and she stood ready. When it opened a crack, Agnes Dupree poked her head out and Emily was caught off guard. Lewis's mum had always been anxious looking but now she was hollow-cheeked and aged beyond her years.

'Is Lewis in?' Emily enquired.

Agnes nodded and cranked open the door wide enough for Emily to slip in. It was hard to see her looking so thin and bedraggled, and even on Christmas day the old skirt that she wore was frayed at the hem. 'Lewis?' Agnes called from the bottom of the stairs, 'Lewis.'

The soft thump of someone getting out of bed in bare feet was followed by his shouting down, 'What?'

'It's me,' Emily called up, 'I need to see you.'

There was movement, and then after a few moments he appeared at the top of the stairs with his shirt untucked and his hair stood up on end. They stood looking at each other for a few moments before Lewis came down.

'I'll just get my coat,' he said, wandering into the sitting room. She could hear the low rumble of his father's voice and then Lewis reappeared in his coat and cap and shoved his feet into the boots that were waiting by the door.

It was freezing outside and their breath mingled in steaming clouds as they walked. 'What do you want?' he croaked, slipping a cigarette out of his pack and lighting up.

'I just wanted to make sure you were all right. You looked like you were in a bit of a bad state last night.'

'When was that?' he said.

'When I was on the way to church, you tried to speak to me.'

He sighed out a lungful of smoke and his hand went up to his forehead. 'I'm sorry about that, I don't even remember – I was out with Stan and he'd been buying round after round.'

'Listen, I understand. I know that you need to let off steam… But I did think that you might have called by to see Jane, given that it's Christmas Day.'

He straightened up instantly and squared his shoulders. 'What do you mean?'

'Well, she is your daughter, I thought you might have brought her a present?'

He spat on the floor and then took another drag of his cigarette. 'So that's it, is it? You just wanted to come over here and give me grief.'

She stopped in her tracks and turned to look him straight in the eye. 'No, of course not,' she said. 'I just thought you might have wanted to see her, that's all.'

He took a final deep drag on his cigarette. 'Well, I know she'll be just fine with you lot and like you said, it's better for her to be there with you than—' He gestured miserably back to his house.

'But that doesn't stop *you* coming over to see us, does it?'

'You've always got an answer for everything, haven't you?' he snapped.

She was about to speak, when he grabbed her and pushed her back against the rough stone wall that surrounded the church. He crushed himself against her, stale beer on his breath, and his bristled chin scraped against her mouth as he tried to kiss her. She turned her face away, pushing hard to get him off her.

'Just as I thought,' he sneered. 'If it wasn't for that child, you'd have run a mile.'

He was still standing close, breathing heavily. She pushed him again and managed to slip out of his grasp.

'Well, we'll see about that,' he shouted, as she walked quickly away, her face still stinging. 'As you just said, she is *my* daughter!'

Emily knew that she'd have to collect herself before she went back into the house, otherwise her sisters would be straight round there to Lewis and then there would probably be even more trouble. She wiped her face with her handkerchief and pulled her coat and hat straight, taking a few deep, shaky breaths before she pushed open the back door.

Lizzie was at the kitchen table, her blonde hair glowing like a halo in the light of the lamp. 'How did you get on?' she asked, a piece of turkey halfway to her mouth.

'Bit of a waste of time,' Emily said, trying to slip by without any further investigation.

Lizzie was straight up, standing in her way. 'Your face is all red, like you've been slapped, what's been going on?'

'He didn't hurt me, not really,' she said. 'He just tried to kiss me, that's all.'

She saw Lizzie's eyes narrow, aware that there was more to it than that, and she didn't seem ready to let it go. But then they both heard the sound of Jane calling from upstairs and the moment moved on. 'I'll go,' said Lizzie. 'She's already calling me Aunty Lizzie.'

Emily's hand was still shaking as she poured herself a big glass of sherry. She moved slowly to the chair next to the stove. Sitting with the glass in her hand, she shuddered – the smell of him was still clinging to her. She lifted the glass and downed the contents in three mouthfuls, wiping her hand across her mouth and feeling better as the sherry warmed her. Her hand was steady now and the sounds of her family in the next room lifted her spirits, reminding her how much support she had here, compared to Lewis. She wasn't ready to give up on him just yet, there had to be remnants of the Lewis that she'd once known somewhere inside of the man who had just accosted her. She just didn't know whether or not she would ever be able to find them.

CHAPTER 18

It was a magical awakening the next day. The wind had picked up overnight and the snow had started to fall and the whole village had become clean and new, covered by a thick layer of snow. There were still some flakes falling as the Burdon sisters gathered in the kitchen and Lizzie flung open the back door, pushing over the small drift of snow on the step with her foot. They'd grown up with icy cold winters, and they were all eager to be outside, especially now that they had Jane.

Wrapped up well, they giggled and slid away from the house. Emily was carrying Jane and the little girl was holding out her hands, opening her mouth to let the snowflakes fall on her tongue. 'Snow,' she kept saying, 'snow!' The flakes caught like sparkles in her dark curly hair. Emily looked up to the sky and felt them falling gentle on her face, like a benediction.

Lizzie came running past, slipping and almost falling, and she plunged her hands into the snow, making a huge snowball that she threw straight at Alice who was progressing step by step, not risking a slip. Alice growled and turned around with a loose ball of snow in both hands that fell apart as she tried to retaliate. Lizzie was circling now, shrieking with laughter. She threw another at Alice and then Emily felt one hit the side of her head, cold ice falling down the neck of her coat. Jane was laughing as Emily put her down knee-deep in the snow so that she could chase after Lizzie, but her sister was too quick as always and had already landed another shot on Emily's back.

After the first flurry of snowballs, they all trudged to the village green, finding a spot where they could make a snowman. Alice worked on the beginnings of the body and Jane helped her roll a big ball of snow, giggling with joy, and no sign of the cold hitting her yet.

The village children and some grown-ups were out and there were shrieks of laughter all around the village green. A fat snowman already stood on the plinth of the stone cross, wearing an extravagant hat that Emily was sure that she'd seen the vicar's wife wearing at the carol service the other evening.

*

On the other side of the green, Lewis was lying flat on his bed watching a curl of smoke drift up to the nicotine-stained ceiling. His curtains were open, and he could see the brightness of the light reflecting off the snow and hear the sound of the children, but he'd woken shouting from one of his dreams, like he did most mornings, and he didn't have the energy to get up. He tried to blot out the nightmare with every drag of his cigarette, but even now, above the joyful cries of the children outside, he could still hear the terrified scream of a soldier, crying out for help…

He'd been standing beside his mate Jim, waiting to go over the top. They'd been laughing about something, sharing a cigarette; they hadn't even heard the shell coming above the noise of gunfire. By some miracle, Lewis had been thrown clear, leaving him choking on dust and clawing with his hands, pulling away rubble, trying to find his best mate.

Jim had been screaming when Lewis pulled him out and the skin on one side of his face was hanging loose. There had been a lot of blood pouring from his chest and Lewis could feel it sticky on his hands. He'd hoisted Jim on his shoulder and run with him, screeching with pain at every jolt. But all Lewis could think was that he had to keep going, no matter how hard Jim shouted, he had to get him to a first aid post. He ran and ran but by the time he got Jim onto a stretcher, he had fallen silent. It was too late. Lewis still felt it in the pit of his stomach, and he could hear the stretcher bearer's voice telling him that Jim was a goner as soon as he got hit. That he should just have left him in the trench, tried to make him comfortable, instead of putting him through hell just to get him to the first aid post. Lewis had cried harder that day than he'd ever done in his whole life.

He groaned and sat up, reaching over to stub out his cigarette in the overflowing ash tray. Slaked with sweat and still in his shirt, he sat at the side of the bed for a few moments, running a hand over his face, feeling the rough stubble on his chin. He was tempted to light up another ciggy but then a shriek from a child prompted him to stand up and stretch his sore muscles. Pulling aside the yellowing net curtain, he scratched the ice off the inside of a windowpane and looked out. The light was so bright at first that it hurt his eyes but as soon as he saw the children playing in the snow it made his mouth twist into the semblance of a smile.

A fat snowman stood at the base of the stone cross and he could see a woman and a dark-haired child there, looking closer, he could tell that it was Emily and Jane. Seeing them, part of the picture postcard scene, made him ache with something that he couldn't even name. He pressed his forehead closer to the glass, trying to get a better look, but they'd turned their backs now and they were trudging through the deep snow back towards the shop.

Lewis turned away, feeling the coldness of the room for the first time, as if he'd only just woken up. He reached for a thick jumper and pulled it on over his shirt. His trousers were lying on the floor and he had them on in moments, flinching as the cold, damp wool hit his skin. He was feeling agitated now, anxious to get out in the snow, wanting to catch Emily and the child before they went back indoors.

Just as he finished lacing his boots, there was a heavy knock at the front door, 'Lewis,' a man's voice shouted. It sounded like one of the neighbouring farmer's sons – Robert Parkinson, or one of his brothers.

He ran down the stairs, his boots hammering on the bare wood. It was Robert, leaning against the door jamb. 'We need a bit of muscle,' he said, his slow smile lighting up a face made ruddy by outdoor work. 'The roads are blocked with snow and we're looking for volunteers to help dig out so we can get the milk churns to town.'

'I'm up for it.' Lewis grinned, suddenly taken with the idea of joining the gang, all thought of catching up to Emily instantly gone. He'd never been asked to dig before, prior to the war he'd been busy in the forge, and they'd always had plenty of hands. But now, with two young men who he'd been at school with killed in the trenches and others who hadn't yet returned from military hospitals, they were in need of an extra pair of hands. He'd always liked Robert, a gentle, brooding man with sandy hair, who didn't say much, but liked a pint, so that was another reason for going – they would most likely end up in the pub at the end of the day. There were others in the group waiting outside the forge that he knew well: Ted Barnes and Richard Hall, seasoned farmers who'd dug out after many a snowstorm.

The snow was deep though and big drifts filled the road, in some parts up to the hedge tops. All of the men stood for a few moments with their shovels over their shoulders, looking at the sculpted, dazzling white perfection of it all. As they started to dig, Lewis was glad that he'd worn his thick leather gloves and a good coat – it was freezing cold. The smooth wooden handle of the shovel slid easily through his hands and it felt balanced in his grip. In a few strokes he was into the rhythm of it – all those years of helping to dig trenches had stood him in good stead.

There was the occasional murmur of a conversation but mostly they worked in silence, digging out and chucking the snow to the side. As they got closer to the base of the drift Ted Barnes shouted, 'Go easy with your shovels now, lads!'

Lewis glanced towards Robert, who just smiled and said, 'You'll see.'

With the next stroke of his shovel, Lewis saw a flash of brown fur and a hare's head popped out of the hole. He gasped with surprise as the creature broke free and bounded away over the snow.

Robert was laughing. 'They get caught in the drift if it comes down quick and the warmth of their bodies melts the snow, so they can still breathe. If they get dug out in time, they're still alive.'

There were other men shouting out in front now and he could see two rabbits scurrying out and running free. The sight of these living creatures being dug out, surviving near-death, filled him with emotion. He kept digging, keeping up the rhythm, but he could feel the tears running down his cheeks and in the end it got the better of him and he had to lean on his shovel and let out a sob.

The old-timer digging at his other side stopped for a moment. 'Don't you be worrying lad, you have a good cry if you need to. I was away in the Boer War, I know summat about what you're goin' through.'

Lewis felt like he was gasping for air, like he could fall to his knees. Still gripping his shovel, he took deep breaths, in and out, to try and steady himself. Robert patted his shoulder.

'I'm all right,' he was saying, ready to move on now to the next section, 'I'm all right.'

Later on, in the pub, with pint after pint, Lewis obliterated all trace of what it was that had welled up whilst he was digging. None of the other fellas mentioned it to him, but Robert stayed next to him all night long. And by the end of their drinking session, he was the one to put Lewis over his shoulder and carry him safely home.

CHAPTER 19

'What are you thinking?' asked Maggie, leaning across the table to Emily as they sat at breakfast the next morning.

'About what?'

'About what you're going to do now – with your work, and with Jane.'

Emily had been pushing it out of her mind ever since she'd walked away from the hospital, but she knew that it wasn't going anywhere. She'd taken two weeks leave from work, but what was she going to do after that? Would she go back to London and take Jane with her? She still hadn't been able to reply to James, she simply had no idea how to respond. And she'd had a letter from Alma only yesterday. Grace had fallen sick; it had been terrifying for a few hours until they'd realised that she was just suffering from a bad throat and extreme exhaustion. The good news was that once she was well enough, Grace would be taking a Sister's post on female medical. Flu cases were down, but they were still getting admissions and Sister Montgomery was increasingly stressed and now so fearful of more nurses dropping over with the flu that she'd started insisting that they all gargled with brandy at the beginning of each shift. Needless to say, not many of the staff objected and it gave some of the probationers a warm glow for the rest of the day. Reading between the lines though, Emily could sense Alma's exhaustion and she was even hinting that she might be thinking about heading back to America.

Her mother was still gazing steadily at her across the table. 'I don't know what I should do.' Emily sighed. 'It all keeps going around in my head.'

Her mum reached out a hand. 'It's just that I've been catching a rumour that's going around the village, that you and Lewis will be getting married soon – somebody even mentioned a date.'

'What?' Emily gasped. 'I've hardly seen Lewis since I got back.'

'Well I know that, but you know what this place is like, people like to jump to their own conclusions. I mean, it's not exactly out of line, after all, you and Lewis were childhood sweethearts and as far as we all know you're still engaged to each other.'

Emily felt a flush of irritation. 'People should mind their own business.'

'You try telling that to the rumour-mongers, this kind of story is bread and butter to them. Personally, I think you need more time. I like Lewis well enough, but he hasn't even been near since you came home and I can see that he's not the same young man who went off to war. I'm not expecting you to have all the decisions to hand, Emily, but I do think we need to know what's happening with regard to Jane.'

Emily was nodding, she could only agree. 'Well, I think I'm going to have to give my notice at the hospital. I need to spend time here at home with Jane and I know now that as much as I love my work at the Infirmary, I'm not sure I would want to take her back to London, and Lewis is in no fit state to look after her.'

'We could have Jane,' her mother offered, raising her eyebrows.

'I know you could, but it wouldn't feel right. You've got dad to look after and the shop and I've grown close to her now, I wouldn't be able to leave her behind even if I wanted to. No, I'll write to the hospital today, tell them I'm not coming back... I'll look for work up here, close to home. The whole world needs nurses right now; I should be able to find something.'

Maggie was smiling, delighted.

'Well, if that's the case, then maybe I should tell you something else… You know that cottage on the row next door, the one that Miss Lindley has lived in for ever? Well, she's very frail now and she's just moved out and gone to live with her sister. It's coming up for rent… and I've already mentioned your name as a potential tenant!'

'Mum!' Emily laughed.

'Well, it wouldn't have mattered if you'd said you were going back to London, I'd just have said you'd changed your mind. Anyway, it needs a good clean and a lick of paint but it would be a lovely little home for you and Jane – it's got a yard at the back where she can play safely and two bedrooms. And if you and Lewis do get married, then it would be ideal.'

Emily felt her chest tighten at the thought of sharing any space with Lewis. But she knew it would be perfect for Jane. Miss Lindley, a retired schoolteacher, had always been a kindly person. She'd often invited the village children in for tea and cakes, and it was a very cosy little cottage.

'Yes, of course, it would be perfect.'

'Well, that's good,' her mother said, rummaging in her apron pocket and producing a large iron key. 'Because I've got this, so that you can go in and have a look round.'

Within fifteen minutes, Emily was inserting the key into the paint-chipped wooden door of the cottage, leaving the firm imprint of her boots in the scattering of snow on the stone step. As she struggled to make the key catch inside the ancient lock, an icy breeze picked up and blew sprinkles of snow at her back. She stood firm, feeling the lock turn at last, almost falling in through the door as it creaked open. Met by the strong smell of mildew and soot, she left the door open to let some air in. It was damp inside the cottage and a thin layer of dust covered everything, but she'd already fallen in love with the pattern of coloured tiles in the narrow hallway and the black-leaded stove in the kitchen. The light was coming in through a small sash window that looked out over the yard, and a pile of snow on the sill outside gave the whole place a fairy-tale feel. She scratched off a circle of ice, pressing close to peer out. The yard was covered in snow but she could see the walls of the privy and a neat washing line running across. Her mum had been right, it was big enough for Jane to play and there was a wooden gate at the back which she knew led out into the fields that surrounded the village.

The stairs creaked as she went up and some dark green wallpaper was already peeling away at the seams. The wood of the stairs was well polished though, beneath the dust.

Glancing into the small bedroom that looked over the yard, Emily could already picture a small bed for Jane and the brightness that a lick of paint would bring. The sun would come up at this side of the property; it would be lovely in here in the morning. A bigger bedroom still contained an iron double-bed frame with an ornamental brass heart entwined with flowers at the head. She sniffed, she didn't think she'd be needing that any time soon… Then again, as far as she could recall, neither did old Miss Lindley. Emily ran a hand over the frame; it was in good condition and looked like it had been custom made. She might ask if she could keep it, even if she was here on her own, it would be nice to have a big bed so that Jane could come in and snuggle up. The dark green velvet curtains were dusty and threadbare and they would definitely need replacing. She scraped away the ice from inside one of the windowpanes and glanced out at the village green. She could see the shape of someone approaching – her heart jumped a beat – it was Lewis and he was heading straight for the cottage.

She ran down the stairs, wanting to get there and shut the door before he could get in. But she was too late and he was already striding in, muffled up in a thick coat with his breath steaming thick in the air.

'So it's right then?' he said, his eyes boring into hers.

'What do you mean?' she replied, knowing full well that he must have heard on the grapevine that she was interested in renting the cottage.

'That you're thinking of coming here, without any mention of me, or our engagement, or what's going to happen to Jane.'

She knew that she needed to keep her voice steady, after all Lewis was Jane's legal guardian. She took a deep shaky breath. 'I've only just found out about it.'

'Why didn't you ask me to come as well?'

She took a moment, trying to take the best tack. 'I've been a bit worried about you Lewis, you haven't really been yourself.'

He barked out a harsh laugh. 'Have you any idea what we went through, out there, in France?'

She felt shame-faced now. 'No, of course not, but I did see the injuries and the shell shock that those injured men had on the ward.'

He snorted. 'Shell shock!' And then he leant in and shouted, 'You try holding onto your best mate as he dies in your arms.'

If he'd been a patient, Emily would have taken some time to calm him down, but this was Lewis and he was here, screaming in her face, and all she wanted to do was scream back at him that yes, she did know what it felt like to have your best friend die in your arms.

Emily could feel her heart pounding; she was angry but also scared of him.

He was glaring at her. 'Anyway, I'm thinking that we should get on and set a date for the wedding.'

'What?' she spat, no longer able to control herself.

'You heard me,' he said, stepping closer, breathing heavily now.

'But you haven't made any effort to see me since we got home and you haven't shown any interest in getting to know your daughter.'

Lewis snarled. 'I've had my own business to attend to and your job is to remember that we're engaged to be married.'

She felt a wave of rage swell in her throat, making her gasp. 'Oh, you mean, engaged to be married, like you were with Lydia?'

He grabbed her, pushing her back against the wall; her feet were slipping on the coloured tiles. She could feel the strength of him and his breath was sour in her face. She had no chance of breaking free; her collar was tight around her neck as he held the lapels of her coat, bunched up in his hand.

'I told you, she meant nothing to me,' he growled.

She could feel his body hard against her, his eyes were wide and she knew that he was going to try and kiss her again. She turned her face away but with his free hand he forced her to face him, his fingers digging into her cheeks. She used both hands, trying to punch him, but the blows glanced off his thick coat and he had her pinned against the wall. She could feel her heart hammering in her chest, knowing that once he kissed her, he wouldn't stop there…

Terrified now, she tried again to struggle free, but he had her pinned to the wall. He was laughing, pushing harder against her. She tried to turn her face away but still he had her held. As he came that bit closer and pressed his dry lips against her mouth, she felt her stomach heave. His mouth was rough, demanding, and it sent a shot of pure fury through her body. She kept her lips firmly closed, determined not to give any sign of yielding.

He drew back, an unasked question on his face.

'I don't want you any more, Lewis.'

She saw his eyes snap with fury and knew that her words had only made things worse. He tightened his grip on her and she could hardly breathe now.

'Lewis!' called Maggie's outraged voice.

Emily saw him switch round and as he let go of her instantly, she almost fell to the ground. Growling, he stalked away. Relief flooded her body, but just as he was pushing his way out of the door, she saw that Maggie had Jane beside her. In that split second, Emily knew exactly what Lewis was going to do. She shouted out at the same moment as he ducked down and scooped Jane up. Instantly, the little girl was screaming and kicking in his arms, but he carried on walking and didn't even look back. Maggie seemed rooted to the spot, shouting after him. Emily was running now, her lungs burning with the ice-cold air. Her feet were slipping and she fell over but she clawed her way back up and she took off after him again. Only to see the door of his house slamming shut behind him.

Emily hammered on the door, hearing the sound of raised voices inside – Agnes was shouting. Her heart twisted when she heard the pitiful wails, as Jane continued to cry. Rattling the door now, increasingly desperate, she tried to shake it loose but it was locked firmly.

Seeing a glow of light from the forge next door, she had no choice but to go in and try to reason with Frank. He was there in his leather apron, using a pair of long-handled tongs to pull a white-hot piece of metal out of the coals, his face bright red and running with sweat. She watched, feeling another wave of anger swell in her throat, as he took the metal across to the anvil and started to hammer it, the muscles rippling on his bare arm. Agonisingly, she knew that she would have to wait until he was finished. As the time went, she could feel beads of sweat forming on her forehead.

Only when he had stopped hammering did he glance up, scowl and then shout, 'What do you want?'

'I need to talk to you about Lewis!' she shouted back.

Frank shrugged, about to dismiss her.

She walked right up to the anvil. 'He has taken Jane, snatched her away, she is screaming and crying now next door, in your house.'

He shrugged again, leaning in so close that she could see his bloodshot eyes and smell the sweat on him. 'Lewis has every right to take the child, she is his daughter.'

Emily's heart was clenched like a fist, she was ready to fight, and she opened her mouth to shout a demand. But then it struck her afresh – he was right, in a court of law Lewis was the legal guardian. But they weren't in a court right now and Jane was in terrible distress, so there was no way that she was backing down. She didn't flinch as they stood eyeball to eyeball, and when her words came, she made sure that they were said with force. 'I want that child back today, and if it doesn't happen, I will be back here with others and we will break down your door.'

Frank smirked then and she knew that he was goading her. It would be a mistake to take it any further. Despite all of her instincts, she would have to withdraw, hoping and praying that Lewis would make sure that Jane was safe.

Her mother was waiting outside the forge and she was crying. 'I'm so sorry, I had no idea that he was going to take her.'

'It's not your fault, if not then, he would have found some way.'

Emily put her arm around her mother, helping her back across the snow, going straight into the shop so that they could share the news with Lizzie and Alice. Lizzie was behind the counter, weighing out some flour. She put down the scoop that was mid-way to the scales and stripped off her apron, ready to go over to the forge.

Alice grabbed her arm. 'No, stop, we need to do this peacefully, just imagine how any kind of commotion would frighten Jane.'

'She's right,' said Maggie, 'and I think there is another way… I'm going back over there now and I'm going to speak to Agnes. If she won't open the door I'll shout through, make sure she hears me. We were at school together, I helped her out many times when she was struggling with Frank, she has to listen to me.'

They all agreed that it was worth a try and Emily moved to go with her.

'No,' said Maggie firmly, 'this is just between me and Agnes.'

It felt like an age before she was back, looking pale and exhausted, and needing to lean on the shop counter. 'She wouldn't open the door, but I shouted through and I could sense that she was listening. She didn't give me an answer, but I kept repeating it, begging her to do something. And at least Jane was quiet…' Her mother was crying now and Emily helped her back through into the kitchen.

'I'll put the kettle on,' Emily said quietly.

They both sat silent at the table; even Rusty was unsettled and pacing back and forth, meowing. 'He's missing her,' sniffed Maggie, getting up to let him out through the back door. Emily sighed heavily, she couldn't find any words, there was nothing that she could say or do.

Hearing the cat meowing again at the door, Emily got up to let him back in, her head feeling heavy on her shoulders.

Rusty shot in and then Emily cried out. There was Agnes with Jane in her arms. Agnes came to a halt, standing thin and dishevelled in her apron. 'I'm so sorry,' she said, 'Lewis had no right to do what he did, scaring her like that but I promise you, he didn't harm a hair on her head.'

Emily wiped at her wet face with the flat of her hand and immediately opened her arms to receive the little girl, her eyes red-rimmed and cheeks flushed from too much crying.

Agnes brushed back some straggles of hair from her face and then she stood helplessly, her head bowed. Emily heard her sigh and then she made to turn.

'No, don't go,' Emily pleaded, 'come in and sit for a while, have a cup of tea.'

'Yes, Agnes, please come in,' said Maggie, standing at the door now.

Agnes looked up and Emily could see that she was about to shake her head but Maggie walked out of the house and took her arm, thanking her for bringing Jane home. Warily, Agnes allowed herself to be led the few steps up to the door but she stopped dead at the threshold, gazing in at the unfamiliar space beyond. 'Come on,' said Maggie, 'it's a long while since you sat at our table. It's time you came back.'

Agnes gave a single nod and then she started to smile, taking one step and then another until she was right in the kitchen and ready to sit down at the kitchen table. Emily put Jane down next to Agnes.

'This is my cat,' the little girl said, reaching for her hand, pointing at Rusty who'd reclaimed his place in front of the fire. As Agnes crouched down beside her, stroking the cat, Emily heard Maggie breathe out a sigh and they exchanged a smile.

Once they were all sat around the table, Agnes started to speak as if the words had been held back for far too long. 'Lewis hasn't been right since he got back, especially this time – he's been shouting out and crying in his sleep, and every time I've tried to ask him anything, he's bitten my head off. When I saw him coming through the door with the little girl, and she was screaming, I knew that I had to do something. I swore that no other child was going to be badly treated in my house.'

Agnes was breathing heavily, lost in her thoughts, and when she looked up, she had tears in her eyes. 'I know, sometimes it's too late to go back and make things right, but I wasn't going to stand by and let any harm come to Jane. I could see, though, that Lewis was already regretting what he'd done. I mean that child – she is strong and she can scream, and the look on her face. He was holding her at arm's length, like she was some spitting cat. Anyway, as soon as he put her down, I picked her up and took her away to the kitchen.

'I heard him running up the stairs and then he was bumping around in his room for quite a while. When he came down, his bag was packed and he was ready to go out of the door.'

Agnes took a shaky breath and her voice quivered on the edge of tears as she began to speak again. 'I think he would have gone without even saying goodbye if I hadn't heard him. He said, *I can't do this, I have to go*, and he looked at Jane, as if he was in agony, and then he pulled open the door and walked away without a backward glance.'

Emily reached a hand out to Agnes. She had long realised that the Lewis she'd known had already gone, but seeing his mother suffering now, it made her want to cry. 'Where has he gone? Do you know?' she asked eventually.

Agnes sighed and shook her head. 'He wouldn't say, but he'd packed all of his things in his army bag as if he was going off again, back to the war. He's been seeing quite a bit of Stan, from the next village, so he might have gone somewhere with him… It's for the best, Frank is a brute, he would never have let Lewis rest… It's for the best.'

Emily could only agree, and she couldn't help but feel the relief of knowing that Lewis didn't seem to have any intention of ever coming back. 'Are you going to be all right though, on your own with Frank?'

Agnes pushed back her hair from her face. 'Well, rightly or wrongly, I've lived with him all these years. And if I'm not all right,' she said, with the beginnings of a glint in her eye, 'I'll be straight over here to let you both know.'

'You do that, Agnes,' said Maggie. 'We can get the police on him if he tries anything.'

Agnes shrugged, she seemed not to care, but she was reaching out a hand to Jane. 'And you, young lady, we had a little chat didn't we when you were at my house? And we went to look at the kittens.'

Jane was giggling. 'I picked one,' she said, her eyes gleaming. 'Yes you did, and you called him Bobby, didn't you?'

Maggie and Emily exchanged a glance. They were both thinking the same thing – it seemed that Jane now had another grandmother, and that was the best thing ever for any little girl.

CHAPTER 20

It was late February and early spring had come to the village with pale yellow sun and clusters of snowdrops on the village green. A union flag had been draped over the stone cross and a piece of oak board, cut carefully with bevelled edges, had been placed there with the names of the village boys who'd been lost in the war painted in black. Even though the sky was clear there was still a nip in the air and as Emily stood at the back door of her cottage, looking out over the fields, the trees seemed to breathe and pulse in the light wind.

She'd been cleaning all day, removing the final layer of dust after the decorating had been done and the furniture had been set in place. She removed her apron, feeling a tingle as her work sore hands caught the rough fabric. It was time to move in.

She walked into the kitchen, standing in the middle of the room with her hands on her hips. The room was warm and cheerful; she'd had the stove lit all day to air through and a small, well-scrubbed deal table stood in pride of place with two mismatched chairs, one at either side. Maggie had taken Jane out for a walk this morning and they'd come back with a posy of snowdrops that now sat in a glass bottle, square in the middle.

Walking by the comfortable settle along the back wall of the kitchen, she passed through into the narrow hallway, smiling with pleasure at the blue and orange floor tiles – they were almost identical to those in the Infirmary chapel. With that thought came a reminder that she needed to write to Alma. In her most recent letter, she'd told Emily that Bill Steadman had called by the hospital with his two boys, looking for Emily, and he had been disappointed to hear that she wasn't coming back to London. Alma had reported that he seemed to be managing well and the boys were keeping him going. Grace had started a session for mothers in a local church hall and she was providing tea and cake and giving out food parcels for the needy ones. And there were now two women doctors at the Infirmary – the first ever appointed. She'd also said that flu cases were down in London and, she was even thinking about taking some time off to make a trip up north.

Emily still couldn't work out if there was anything going on between Alma and James – Alma often mentioned him in her letters, but it was usually work-related. And it all seemed so long ago now, she was sure that he would have moved on from what he'd written in his letter that she'd read and re-read so many times. Once she'd started working on the house, she'd stashed the letter away in her special box of keepsakes, telling herself very firmly that his words were probably driven by overwork and exhaustion. Plus, given that she'd never been able to construct a reply – well, he must have drawn his own conclusion from that. So many times she'd started to write, but every time she had scrunched up the piece of paper and thrown it to the back of the fire.

At least she was free of Lewis now, and even if he did show his face back here, there wasn't any way that she would become involved with him again. She would fight him at every turn if he tried to take Jane, and now that they had Agnes on their side, it was unlikely that he'd get far. Everybody in the village knew how disturbed Lewis had been – not that it was his fault, but when it came to the raising of a child, the cause didn't matter. If a person wasn't fit to take charge, they weren't fit, and that was it really.

Climbing the stairs, Emily checked each of the bedrooms – Jane's small room was painted in pale yellow, and hers was a light blue, the colour of a blackbird's egg. She'd been right to keep the cast iron bed; it had cleaned up beautifully. The ornate brass heart and flowers now gleamed with polish, and it all looked very inviting with the brand-new double patchwork quilt that Alice and Lizzie had made as a housewarming gift. She loved this room with its oak floorboards and stripped wood dresser, she knew that she was going to be very happy here. More so because she'd been devising a plan to set up a small clinic – she'd been asked so many times for medical advice on various ailments by a number of villagers and after she'd given first aid for a finger severed at the local sawmill and a nasty head wound received by a falling slate, word had got round that she knew her stuff.

The tiny downstairs room by the front door that had served Miss Lindley as a parlour had been lime washed and Emily had used most of her savings to buy a range of medicines and equipment and install a couch. With the doctor and the district nurses in the nearby town snowed under with work and still some flu cases, she would have enough paying customers to make a living. She'd already rooted out her hospital badge and Maggie had pinned it to a piece of board so that she could display it on the clinic wall, alongside the certificate that the Infirmary had sent soon after she'd submitted her notice. It would all be perfect.

As she clattered down the stairs, she heard her mother at the door, shouting, 'Emily,' and then with a rising note of panic in her voice, 'Emily! Come quick, it's Lizzie, she can't breathe properly.'

Emily started to run. 'Where is she, in the shop?'

'We've brought her through to the kitchen.'

Emily ran fast, leaving her mother behind. Even from outside the kitchen door she could hear the sound of her sister. The high-pitched wheeze set her teeth on edge, taking her straight back to Lucy fighting for breath. Emily felt a stab of grief, still strong enough to pierce her heart.

'Tell me what happened,' she called to Alice, as she came running into the kitchen.

'She said she was feeling a bit sickly this morning and she didn't have much breakfast, and then she started to get shivery. I checked her and she was hot. Later on, she came over all tired and said that her bones were aching, so I got her to sit down. Then her chest started to feel tight and she was making this horrible noise—' Alice had dissolved into tears, saying something about a man with a cough who'd been in the shop last week, some stranger, and how she should have told him to stand outside. Emily was only half-listening as she rapidly assessed Lizzie. She put the back of her hand against her forehead – it was burning hot, and her radial pulse was rapid and bounding against her fingers.

'Lizzie,' she called, giving her shoulder a shake.

Lizzie opened her eyes and she tried to speak, but she wasn't making much sense. Emily's mouth was dry and she could feel her heart pounding against her ribs. She took a moment to collect herself. Seeing her mother standing with little Jane, their eyes wide with fear, she knew that she had to be calm and she had to take charge.

'Mum, I want you to take Jane through into the sitting room with Dad, and Alice, I need you to help me carry Lizzie back to the cottage, so that I can treat her.' Already, she was running through a check list in her head. 'We'll have to carry her in the chair, Alice, can you manage one side if I take the other?' They moved as quickly as they could; Emily knew it wasn't ideal but it would be easier to nurse her in the treatment room and she wanted to isolate her immediately from the rest of the family.

'Thank goodness she's the skinniest one of the family,' Alice uttered, already out of breath with the exertion as they edged their sister in through the front door of the cottage.

'Bring her in here,' ordered Emily, indicating the clinic room directly to the left, 'we'll put her on the couch. Both of them were out of breath by the time they had her propped up with some pillows behind her. 'I need you to help me prepare things, Alice, and then you have to go back home, I want to minimise your risk of catching it.'

'But what about you?'

'I've nursed hundreds of cases, I must be resistant by now, and before the worst of it came, I think I caught a mild dose, so it's very unlikely that I'm going to fall victim to it now.'

Emily was already unbuttoning Lizzie's blouse. 'Help me get her stripped down to her petticoat, that in itself will help cool her down, and then, see that bowl over there, go and get me some cool water so I can tepid sponge her. Oh, and if you could fill the glass jug with cold water, I can start to get some fluid inside her.'

As soon as Alice returned, Emily was ready to give more instruction. 'The only other thing I need you to do is light the fire in here for me – there are plenty of sticks and some coal outside in the yard – I want to try a steam kettle to loosen her chest.'

Once Alice had lit the fire, Emily spoke clearly, 'You must go now. This thing can spread rapidly, I don't want any of you near here. Wash your hands with the carbolic soap in the kitchen, there's a nail brush there so you can scrub them thoroughly.' Seeing her sister linger, Emily pleaded, 'Go, go. This is important… And if any of you fall sick, come here to me, do you understand?'

Alice nodded and turned wearily.

Emily wanted to call after her, tell her not to worry, that Lizzie would be fine, but she'd seen this disease, she knew what could happen.

After the tepid sponging, Emily brought out her mercury thermometer from the cupboard and placed it under Lizzie's arm. Her temperature was still dangerously high, so Emily would have to leave the cool flannels in place and be sure to keep replacing them.

'Lizzie,' she called, giving her a shake, 'I need you to drink.'

Lizzie opened her eyes and murmured. Emily brought the cup to her lips and gently poured some water in. To Emily's relief, she saw her swallow, and then she took some more. She would crush up two aspirin to give with the next drink, that would help bring her fever down.

Lizzie's breath was rasping and Emily took her new stethoscope to listen to her chest. This was something that James had taught her during the worst of it, at the Infirmary. She moved the stethoscope around, remembering what he'd said as she listened for abnormal bubbling or crackling sounds. She could almost hear his voice in her head as she did so. Thankfully, Lizzie's chest was clear – so far. She had high hopes that the steam kettle might help loosen the secretions and help Lizzie expectorate. Yet she'd seen so many flu victims coughing and coughing until they brought up blood. *That won't happen to Lizzie,* she told herself as she kept an eagle eye on the colour of her sister's lips and her fingertips, dreading to see any sign of cyanotic blue.

As the steam filled the room, she heard a change in Lizzie's breathing; maybe it was wishful thinking but she was sure that it was less strident and she now seemed more comfortable. Emily saw her opportunity and went up the stairs to bring down a chair from Jane's room and the blankets off her bed – it was going to be a long night of keeping vigil and she knew that she needed to get as much rest as she could.

She kept up her routines – sponging, giving fluids, steaming, checking temperature and pulse and listening to her chest. She would be able to give two more aspirin in due course but, beyond that, there was nothing else that she could do except regularly adjust Lizzie's position on the couch to try and prevent fluid from settling on her lungs. As the evening wore on into night, to stay awake she started telling Lizzie about some of her escapades at the Infirmary – stories of her and Lucy as probationers on the wards and laughing till their ribs ached as they danced in Lucy's room to the portable gramophone; and, of course, all of her reprimands and trips to the Infirmary chapel. She even told her about seeing James for the first time in the corridor outside the doctors' mess and what had happened between them – she left nothing out and even related the incident with James and Alma that night at the back of the hospital.

In the early hours of the morning, there was a change in the rhythm of Lizzie's breathing. Emily jumped and grabbed Lizzie by the shoulders, pulling her forward, rubbing her back, patting her, almost in tears as her sister convulsed and continued to wheeze. Then Lizzie coughed again, choking with it, and something loosened. Emily listened, holding her breath, when Lizzie drew in more air; whatever obstruction there'd been, it had shifted. Bringing the lamp closer, she felt sick to her stomach as she checked Lizzie's fingertips, lips and ears for cyanosis, panicking at first because in the dull glow of the lamp, her lips looked blue. When at last she was reassured that they were pink and she'd checked and rechecked her fingertips, she collapsed back in the chair, holding back the tears.

It was time again to refill the steam kettle and as she clattered back into the room, she saw Lizzie opening her eyes. 'Where am I?' she said, trying to sit up.

'You're at my house,' Emily consoled, an ache in her heart, just hearing the sound of Lizzie's voice. 'I've been looking after you… I think you've got the Spanish flu.'

'Oh no,' croaked Lizzie, 'I was meant to be going to a dance on Saturday.'

Emily felt a bubble of laughter rising in her chest; she couldn't control it and then Lizzie was chuckling as well.

'Anyway,' her sister said, 'who is this James you've been going on about all night long?'

Emily could have hugged her and hugged her, but she didn't want to set her off coughing again, so instead she reached out and took her hand. 'I'll tell you more about that in due course. Right now, all that matters is that you're feeling better.'

CHAPTER 21

Emily opened the curtains so that she could see the first light come. Although still heavy with tiredness, she had a buzz of adrenaline through her body, which sent a tingle from her head to her toes. Lizzie was sleeping peacefully, just the faintest catch in her breathing, but the fever had subsided – her sister's face was pale now with a mere flush of pink. Emily regularly picked up her wrist to check her pulse – no longer galloping but steady with a normal volume.

Even though it was too early to say for sure that the flu had passed through Lizzie's body and would definitely not return, Emily brimmed with pure joy. Joy for the life that was saved. She still thought about Lucy every single day, often waking to the sound of her tap on the door and hearing the ripple of her laughter. For her to be taken so suddenly and so cruelly was still devastating, but she knew that similar losses were shared across the country, across the world. Only yesterday, she'd heard that the figure of those who had fallen to this flu worldwide was somewhere in the region of fifty million, around ten times higher than those killed in the war. It seemed incomprehensible – and she'd been on the front line, seeing the stark reality as the cases poured into the hospital. At the time, they'd all just got on with the work, pulled together, but what an experience… She hoped that no nurse would ever have to see anything like that, ever again.

But she had come through, and right now, with spring on the way, she could feel in her bones that the world was coming out of this terrible time. The flu was beaten and hopefully, soon, it would be gone for good.

Seeing the first rays of sun peeping in through the sash, Emily started to smile. She walked to the window, gazing out at the deserted village. One or two birds were just starting to sing and a cheeky robin with a deep red breast was pecking on the ground right outside her window. The bird lifted his head to look up at her, as if he was trying to tell her something, and then his wings fluttered and he was gone, up and away into the air.

Soon, Alice would be stopping by and Emily would be able to tell her that Lizzie was on the mend. Emily smiled again just thinking about it. As soon as she heard the knock, she ran to open the door.

Alice didn't even need her to say the words. 'Can I see her?' she said, moving straight through when Emily gave her the go ahead.

'Don't get too close,' croaked Lizzie, 'I've got the lurgy.'

But Alice ignored her and took her hand. 'Don't you ever dare do that again… You frightened the living daylights out of me.'

'Well, I probably won't get the Spanish flu again, if that's what you mean, but if I do get another horrible disease, I'll make sure that you're fully involved.'

Alice was laughing and then she was saying excitedly, 'I need to go and tell the others, I won't be long… I'll bring you some breakfast back.'

Not until Emily had her patient moved upstairs and comfortably propped with feather pillows in the cast iron bed, did she start to feel the exhaustion hitting her so hard she staggered to Jane's small bed and collapsed down, falling asleep instantly. She woke with a start to the sound of her mother's voice calling from the bottom of the stairs.

'Can I see the patient?' she was asking.

'Just for a moment,' Emily replied, crawling out of bed, pushing her hair out of her eyes and walking through to the top of the stairs. 'We need to keep the chance of contagion to a minimum'

'Yes, Sister!' her mother said with mock formality as she ascended the stairs.

'And no hugging or kissing!' Emily warned. 'And if you touch her at all, you need to wash your hands.'

'I will, I will.' Her mother stepped quietly around her and into the bedroom. She stood at the bottom of the bed, content to watch the easy breathing of her middle daughter. She looked over to Emily with tears in her eyes. 'You've done a good job, Emily. I'm so proud of you... Word's got out around the village that you're now the local flu expert, as well as everything else.'

'Ha!' laughed Emily, and then her voice was solemn. 'Let's hope we don't see any more cases, I've nursed enough flu to last me more than a lifetime.'

'I should have known this was coming... There was an article in the *Evening Post* the other week, saying that there'd been a resurgence of cases and more deaths in Manchester. Why didn't I think to show it to you?'

'It wouldn't have made any real difference, we've been lucky here all of this time and it was bound to show up at some stage.'

'Even so, I've been racking my brain trying to think where Lizzie caught it. Do you think it was somebody coming into the shop? We have travellers passing through. Or could she have got it at those dances she goes to? She went there again last week, I should have stopped her from going.'

Emily could hear her mother's voice spiralling. 'Look,' she said, 'this is nobody's fault. This particular flu spreads easily and yes, we need to be as careful as we can and keep the windows open and wash our hands, but this can never be the fault of any one individual, it's all of our responsibility, all of the time.'

'When will it end, when will it all end?' Maggie said wearily.

'I don't know for sure, but I've heard reports that the cases that we're seeing now aren't as severe – and I don't know why, but I feel things might be changing for the better.'

Maggie was nodding, but she looked sceptical. She took a deep breath and roused herself. 'Well, I'd best get back – Alice is manning the shop single-handedly and I've left your father in charge of Jane, she'll have him doing all sorts. Thank you again, Emily, without you and your training, I don't know what we'd have done… Oh, and there's this,' she said, turning to hand her a letter. 'It's got a London postmark.'

Emily felt her heart jump a beat, but when she saw the hand-writing, she knew that it was from Alma. She tore it open as soon as her mother departed, and read it through quickly.

'Oh!' she said out loud, halfway down the page, looking out through the window for a moment, and then reading that particular passage over again. Alma wouldn't be coming to the north now, she was heading back to America as soon as possible. She'd met up with an old flame from Richmond and they would be travelling back home together. *He is GORGEOUS and from a tearaway family*, Alma had written, *Aunt Foster would definitely not approve – so that's all to the good then!*

Emily laughed so loudly that Lizzie started to wake up.

In days, Lizzie was ready to move back to the family home and Emily was busy cleaning through the house again, making sure to disinfect the clinic room and launder anything that had come into contact with her patient at the height of the infection. It was ever so satisfying to know that Lizzie was able to get up and about, a bit wobbly on her legs, but well and truly on the mend.

The sun was shining and the sparrows were chirruping in the hedge when Lizzie stepped out of the cottage, a bit shaky, but with Emily at her side. She stood for a few moments, drawing in some big breaths of air before closing her eyes and turning her face to the sky. 'It all seems so fresh and new.' She beamed.

'We don't realise how precious everything is, do we? Not until something happens…'

Jane was ecstatic when she saw them coming in through the back door, jumping up and down on the spot and screeching with so much joy that Rusty shot out of the kitchen like a bolt of lightning. And when Maggie wheeled Charles through and he saw Lizzie, the one single tear that escaped down his cheek, set them all off crying.

CHAPTER 22

The man looked expectant, like the world was at his feet and all he needed to do was explore it. Even so, he had begun to wonder whether walking from the railway station had been the best decision. Some of the narrow country lanes didn't even have names and he found himself regularly consulting his map. But being out in the countryside after so long confined to the city, in the midst of so much sickness, he felt like he could breathe again. And the fresh green fields, the new leaves and the May blossom, made him feel at home.

He strolled over to lean on a five-barred gate, consulting his map once again. He didn't think he had many miles to go now and there was no rush, with no set time… In fact, the person he was visiting didn't even know he was coming. He gazed across the fields, noting the line of the dry-stone walls that formed a border, hugging the contours of the uneven landscape. Some Shorthorn cows with their calves were grazing and two of them lifted their heads, looking at him for a few moments before going back to their grass. In the next field, he could see sheep, small in comparison to those he knew from his own family farm, but they looked strong and the lambs were obviously thriving – two or three were racing around the meadow, kicking their legs in the air.

He felt his connection to the land in the smell of the earth and the warmth of the sun on his face. Gazing back across the field he caught an image of himself back home, cantering through green grass on his favourite chestnut horse, leaving the farmstead behind him. He heard the cry of the gulls and saw again the light on the ocean, knowing that he would go down to the beach and gallop through the surf before he headed home.

A glimmer of movement in the sky caught his attention and brought him back to the present – it was a kestrel, soaring high and then hovering. He continued to gaze, shielding his eyes from the sun as the majestic bird hung in the air. When it plummered like an arrow, straight down to the ground, he felt a thrill go through his body. Instantly, he was on the move again, feeling a prickle of urgency now, needing to get to his destination.

This must be the right village, he thought, seeing a stone cross in the middle of a green. He twisted his map; yes, that seemed to be it. He saw the red glow of a blacksmith's forge and as he passed by, glancing in, he saw a broad-shouldered man with a heavy scowl stop at his work and look up. He nodded a *hello* but the man went straight back to his work without acknowledging him and struck hard at a piece of metal on his anvil.

Seeing a small church to his right, James noted the beauty of its warm stone and simple lines. He would have stopped to have a closer look, maybe gone in through the gate and had a wander round, if he wasn't already looking ahead and starting to feel the urgency of his mission.

At the far end of the village green he saw a stone-built detached property with what looked like a shop front. *That has to be it*, he thought, striding purposefully now. As he walked, the door of a cottage a few doors down from the shop opened, and a young woman with a streak of red in her glossy brown hair stepped out. She was wearing a high-collared white blouse and a black skirt cut just above the ankle, and she had a white apron tied firmly around her waist. He watched admiringly as she guided an elderly man with a bandaged leg carefully out through the door, making sure that he was steady enough to walk with his two sticks.

'Emily!' James called when he could see that her patient was safely on his way. 'Emily.'

*

Emily had sometimes seen hikers coming through the village, often these 'wanderers' were regarded sceptically by the villagers. Any story of one getting stuck in a bog or losing his way and wandering into a field with a bull always made the rounds. But this handsome man, with his blue shirt open at the neck and his pack on his back, seemed to have more purpose, and he knew her name.

He was striding towards her now in his sturdy boots, smiling broadly, and with a shock, she saw his face. Completely thrown – she'd only ever seen him in a suit and tie –she felt her mouth drop open.

'Hello,' James said confidently – he still had the warmest, kindest, blue eyes.

She cleared her throat. 'Hello,' she said, gulping in some more air. 'What are you doing here?'

'I've come to see you…' His accent rolled delightfully over his tongue.

She felt her breath catch in her throat, he was stepping closer now and he was saying, 'Alma told me what happened between you and Lewis… You didn't think that your lack of reply to my letter would put me off, did you?'

'Yes,' she laughed, 'yes, I did.'

'Did you want it to put me off?'

'No, I didn't, but everything was complicated and then, well, I thought that you and Alma were…'

He was shaking his head. 'Whatever made you think that?'

'I saw you together at the back of the hospital one night when it was almost dark. I just assumed…'

He frowned, looking past her for a second, deep in thought.

'Oh, no, that wasn't… She was consoling me, that's all, I'd just had a letter from my family telling me that my brother had had the flu, and he'd pulled through. I was so relieved; I came over all emotional.'

'Oh, I see…'

He was right in front of her now, taking her hand. 'Emily, I meant all of those things I said in that letter. From the first time I saw you in the corridor, when you were with your friend and you were desperately trying to stop her from laughing out loud—'

'Lucy, I was with Lucy,' she murmured, 'and I remember every detail of that moment too.'

She could see his breath coming quickly. 'Emily, I haven't been able to stop thinking about you.'

His words were overwhelming, now that they'd been spoken so boldly, out loud, right there in the village where she'd been born. She felt confused, exposed somehow. Then she caught a flash of longing in his eyes and something shifted in the air between them. Her body prickled with sensation, she opened her mouth to speak but for a split second, no words would come. 'You'd best come in,' she said breathlessly, starting to turn for him to follow. But he grabbed her hand and pulled her close and his arms were around her there and then, out in the open.

Once she felt his lips on her own, she didn't care where they were or who was watching and she carried on kissing him for as long as she needed. And she couldn't be exactly sure, because her head was buzzing with so much anticipation, but she thought that she caught the sound of a cheer and that out of the corner of her eye, she saw someone waving from the shop doorway.

With James inside the cottage, being so tall and confined inside such a small space made him look like a giant. Emily was laughing out loud as she took his hand and led him through to the kitchen.

'This is so quaint, so English,' he was saying, as she removed his backpack and then she had her arms around him again. He smelt of fresh air and his lips tasted of salt, as she revelled in the warmth of his body against her own.

'You might just have to marry me,' she murmured.

'Yes, that's true,' he said, between kisses. 'But I think right now… there is someone knocking at your door.'

'Oh no, it's my next patient!' She laughed, pulling her apron straight. 'Sit right there and don't move, I won't be long.'

As soon as she had the door open, she could see that her patient, Mr Wells, another elderly farmer, was struggling to breathe.

'Do you have any pain?' she asked, steadying him, but he was so breathless he was unable to speak. He clasped a hand to his chest and started to gasp. 'James!' she shouted.

'Right, sir,' James said kindly, 'let's get you sat down, and then I can have a listen to your chest.'

Emily could see the look on the man's face when he saw the tall man with a strange accent, but he was far too breathless to ask any questions.

'This is Dr Cantor, from the St Marylebone Infirmary in London,' Emily said, making the introduction as James led him through carefully. 'In there,' she said, indicating the door to the clinic room.

James glanced inside and commented, 'This is nicely set up.'

'I know,' she replied with a smile, indicating that they should guide Mr Wells to the sturdy, straight-backed chair that stood ready and waiting. The man sighed out with relief as soon as he was sitting and immediately his breathing started to settle. As Emily handed James her stethoscope, she saw the look of appreciation on his face. She had to turn away as he moved the instrument over the man's chest, she was so overjoyed she thought she might burst with excitement. This felt so right that, already, she was making plans in her head – maybe, just maybe, she could persuade James to join her in her country practice…

James looked up at last and removed the stethoscope from his ears. 'Your chest sounds clear enough, but your heart is having a jump about, maybe that's what's making you out of breath.'

'Mr Wells uses digitalis,' Emily offered, as James picked up the man's wrist to feel his pulse.

'Mmm, I'm wondering if we should increase his dose a little, what do you think Nurse Burdon?'

She had been thinking exactly the same thing. After full instructions had been offered to Mr Wells and they had assisted his safe departure, they both stood quietly chatting at the cottage door, feeling the sun on their faces. Hearing a shout, Emily looked to her right – it was her mother, pushing her father in the wheelchair, his arm protectively around Jane who was riding on his knee. Emily stepped out from the cottage, pulling James with her. She could see her mum smiling and then Jane was crying out with delight, shouting and waving.

'It looks like she remembers you,' said Emily. James was laughing, shaking his head, pulling Emily close to his side as they both walked over to the wheelchair. 'This is James,' Emily said, feeling two spots of pink flush her cheeks.

In moments, the door of the shop was opening and Lizzie came running out, closely followed by Alice. The couple were surrounded by everybody talking all at the same time and all that James could do was smile and smile.

Emily looked from one person to another as they all stood together in a group, her heart swelling with pride and happiness. She wished that she could stretch out her arms to embrace James and all of her family, hold them close, all at the same time.

Ever since she'd started her nursing, she'd known that life was precious, a gift that could be taken away in a single breath. But now, after losing Lucy and Lydia and becoming a mother to Jane, she fully understood that love and care were at the centre of all that she did. These were the important threads of life, and in the end, they were the only thing in this world that truly mattered.

A LETTER FROM KATE

I want to say a huge thank you for choosing to read *When the World Stood Still.* If you enjoyed it and want to keep up to date with all my latest releases, just sign up at the following link. Your email address will never be shared and you can unsubscribe at any time.

www.bookouture.com/kate-eastham

In 2020, the world stood still once more due to the COVID-19 pandemic and we witnessed first-hand how fragile our lives can be and how precious a resource the work of our nurses, doctors and key workers is. If ever the world needed to see what professional and dedicated nurses did for a living, this was the time.

With no choice but to let my own nurse registration lapse when I became a full-time carer some years ago, I found myself in a situation where I was contacted by the Nursing and Midwifery Council, asking if I would volunteer to help out during the crisis. Seeing images of nurses in critical care, in accident and emergency, on respiratory wards, doing their absolute best to manage in extraordinary circumstances, my heart was telling me to go out there and help in any way that I could, even though I knew that I had to stay at home to protect my husband who has advanced Parkinson's disease. Surely there was something that I could do?

Like many others forced to shield their loved ones during that first lockdown in the UK, the experience wasn't easy and it was isolating. However, as always, my new job as a writer was the thing that kept me going. In a matter of days after I received the request to re-register as a nurse, my editor was asking if I'd be interested in writing a novel set during the time of the Spanish flu. I didn't even have to think about it – if I couldn't go back to my first profession then maybe I could write about the experience of nursing during a previous pandemic. Immediately, I started the research and found that unlike COVID-19, those at greatest risk from Spanish flu were healthy young adults aged twenty to thirty. It was horrendous and I was moved to tears at times whilst reading some of the historic descriptions.

The nurses of 1918–19 wore cloth masks and aprons and there were no antibiotics or sophisticated medical technologies. The best chance that they could give their patients was through good nursing care and a set of traditional remedies. Without effective protective clothing, my 1918 counterparts were very vulnerable to infection and the records show that nine nurses died at the St Marylebone Infirmary. The medical superintendent, Dr Basil Hood, reported in his notebook that staff were 'going down like ninepins'. He was sad to relate that some of those who lost their lives were 'literally fighting to save their friends and then going down and dying themselves.' He urged them to wear their masks at all times and not to get too close to those coughing but when it came to tending a colleague, many pulled down their masks for fear of distressing a fellow nurse.

Nursing the sick is a universal experience, linked through space as well as time. During our own pandemic, we saw reports from across the world of doctors and nurses in critical care, all united in the fight to save their patients by whatever means possible. Images of exhausted staff with faces marked by wearing protective masks over long shifts without a break, involved with complex technical procedures but also striving to communicate by any means possible with distressed relatives separated from their loved ones. Care staff in residential homes nursing their residents, being there for them and holding a hand when it was impossible for their families to visit. This was an extreme time with added pressures, but this is the work that nurses and care workers do, day in day out, whether there is a pandemic or not. I can only hope that the recognition that they have gained is never forgotten.

Florence Nightingale said that 'every tear one sheds waters some good thing into life'. I'm not sure if this is always entirely true, but I do know that nurses are optimistic. They have to be, because the work can be harrowing and sometimes dispiriting. I've tried to show the resilience and dedication to duty that must have thrived at the St Marylebone Infirmary. And one thing that we can be sure of in these uncertain times is that there is always hope and that the living life that is at the heart of hospitals, hospices and care facilities across the world will always hold fast, whatever happens.

I hope you loved *When the World Stood Still*. If you did, I would be very grateful if you could write a review. I'd love to hear what you think, and it makes such a difference in helping new readers discover my books for the first time.

I love hearing from my readers – you can get in touch on Twitter. Thank you!

All best wishes to you and yours,
Kate Eastham

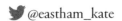 @eastham_kate

ACKNOWLEDGEMENTS

I am indebted as always to the stories that inspire me. From the very start of the research for *When the World Stood Still*, I was moved by the historical accounts of the Spanish flu. Alongside my unique perspective gained from writing during a pandemic, they were key to an understanding of the impact of such a crisis at a time when the world was coming to the end of a devastating world war. Learning of the experiences at the St Marylebone Infirmary was particularly relevant.

I'd like to thank my agent, Judith Murdoch, for her continuing support and advice. Also, Kathryn Taussig and all of the wonderful team at Bookouture for their amazing and very attentive approach.

And, as ever, I would like to thank my family for their love, enthusiasm and for always believing in me.

Finally, I need to mention my father who died suddenly before I was ever able to tell him that I'd found a new job, as a writer. He was the one who gave me the account of the rabbits in the snow. A story passed down by my grandfather who was a farmer, and had dug out with a shovel many times during hard Lancashire winters when the country roads were blocked with snow… and so the stories live on.

Printed in Great Britain
by Amazon